Praise for

THE DARKENING PATH

series

rkly disconcerting high fantasy.
ogen Russell Williams, *Literary Review*

trifying tale of portals into different magical worlds.
holas Tucker, *Independent on Sunday*

nts, dwarfs and magic all bubble in the mix.
uzy Feay, *Financial Times*

ilip Womack is one of the best contemporary authors
children's fantasy.
hilip Reeve

A cracking pace, enigmatic characters and terrifying adversaries.
– Sarah Naughton

Like Alan Garner, Philip Womack takes ancient fairy-tales about searching for a child kidnapped by dark magic and turns it into a haunting adventure exploring love, courage, fear and friendship. Written with sensitivity, intelligence and conviction, it's the kind of classic story readers can't get enough of.
– Amanda Craig

Philip Womack's uncompromising fantasy adventure flies intoxicatingly through a vividly imagined, treacherous and magical world. It's perfect family reading.
– Love Reading 4 Kids

Plenty of horror, plenty of monsters, lots of action ...
– The Mole, ourbookreviewsonline

Philip Womack continues to entrance his readers.
– Julia Eccleshare

The Darkening Path series – a set of books steeped in magic, where people transform into swans, doorways to other worlds open up beneath supermarkets and artefacts in the British Museum hold very special powers . . .
– Abi Elphinstone (moontrug)

Mesmerizing fantasy . . . grips throughout.
– *Parents in Touch*

Kept me hooked from the first page to the last word.
– Sam Harper, age 10, LoveReading4Kids

FANTASTICALLY written fantasy adventure, from the day it arrived it didn't leave my hands. It will capture your imagination from the very first page.
– Rose Heathcote, age 15, Love Reading 4 Kids

For ATAZ

Also available in
The Darkening Path trilogy:

The Broken King
The King's Shadow

Also by Philip Womack:

The Other Book
The Liberators
The Double Axe

THE DARKENING PATH
BOOK THREE

THE KING'S REVENGE

Philip Womack

troika books

Published by TROIKA BOOKS

First published 2016

Troika Books

Well House, Green Lane, Ardleigh CO7 7PD, UK

www.troikabooks.com

A CIP catalogue record for this book is available

from the British Library

ISBN 978-1-909991-30-9

1 2 3 4 5 6 7 8 9 10

Printed in Poland

CONTENTS

⊰⊱ ⊰⊱

PART ONE: THE SILVER KINGDOM

PART TWO: THE CENTRE OF THE WORLDS

PART ONE

THE
SILVER KINGDOM

Chapter One

MADDENED
MAGEHAWKS

FANGS BARED, the royal hound sprang at Simon, its black fur bristling.

Simon ducked sideways and the hound, veiny eyes glaring and nearly as big as he was, flew past him, almost ripping his arm with its long canines. He gagged as he caught its sulphurous stench in his nostrils, but ignored the sensation, and quickly readied himself to lay a blow on the hound's back with his short sword.

But the hound was too fast. It jackknifed, snarling, and pounced with its full might.

The beast crashed into Simon, making him drop

his weapon, which clattered on to the hard floor, and the hound took the opportunity to clamp on to Simon's leg with its jaws. He struggled to push it off, grabbing fistfuls of fur and skin. A jolt of pain rushed through him, and the room started to go dim and faraway, his thoughts slipping from the present moment as he began to lose consciousness.

He'd made a long journey to get to this point, here in the Silver Kingdom, and it all came back to him, parading before his mind's eye in a series of clear images.

Though he could feel the hound worrying at his leg, his eyes began to close, the pain almost overwhelming.

It seemed so long ago now, when his little sister, Anna, had been annoying him back at home in Limerton, on Earth, and he'd said the spell that had called Selenus, the King of the Silver Kingdom, to take her away.

He'd gone on a long quest to rescue her. But when he'd done so, the dying king had sprung a trap, blocking the Way between the worlds, forcing them to remain where they were in the Silver Kingdom.

He'd got this far, though. He wouldn't let a dog, however huge and terrifying, beat him when he'd faced snakes made out of shadows, deadly, shape-shifting knights, and worse.

With a massive effort, Simon gathered all his remaining strength and heaved at the hound, pushing it off and kicking it hard in the stomach.

Yelping in surprise, the hound turned tail and skittered away.

But not for long.

Almost immediately it swirled round and readied itself for the final attack.

Simon tensed. The hound bounced upwards, and caught Simon's leg between its teeth, knocking him to the floor. He scrabbled to fight it off once more.

It was no use. The hound was too big. He was done for.

'Leave him!' A cool voice cut through the air, commanding the hound.

Reluctantly, the hound released Simon's leg, leaving a small, bloodied tear in his trousers. Whimpering with disappointment, it padded over to the side of the room to slump down by its mistress.

There Selena, recently crowned Queen of the Silver Kingdom in place of her father, was watching. With her newly grown horns, which marked her as the queen, curving out of the side of her head, she made a striking figure. Her hair was tied neatly in a plait; a dark, loose gown fell around her, its hem reaching to the wooden floor.

She patted the hound, and it rested its head between its huge front paws, slobbering slightly, and letting out a huge sigh and a big, pink lolling tongue.

'Not your best, Simon,' said Selena sharply. 'We don't know what we're going to be facing. Men, beasts and stranger things. You need to be faster, stronger.'

Simon, panting, nodded. 'I'll get better.'

Flora, who'd been watching anxiously from the other side of the room, came running over to him. 'I thought you did all right,' she said and offered her hand, but he ignored it and got up himself, wincing slightly.

Selena swept to the doors of the training room and unbarred them, calling for attendants, who quickly came bearing bowls of hot, scented water, and a balm that smelled of flowers, and bathed and dressed the bite. Simon thanked them.

'We'll finish for now. We meet in the Central Chamber at the high point of the sun.' Selena strode away, gown billowing, the hound and a clatter of attendants following.

Simon, leaning back on his elbow, looked out at the high window above, at the strange, silver sun that shone during the day in the Silver Kingdom. It had risen and set four times since the green rider Andaria had killed Selenus.

Four days since the king's trap had sprung. Four long days of combat training, of tumbles, scratches, bruises, of sword fighting and hand fighting, training their minds and their muscles for what was to come, all overseen by Selena.

'I don't know what she's expecting, but let's hope we don't have to become martial arts experts to survive,' said Flora sympathetically. 'I mean, I can hardly even climb up a rope.'

'Me neither,' laughed Simon, then laughed even more when Flora performed a spectacularly bad impression of a judo chop.

They walked together through the black glass corridors of the palace of the Queen of the Silver Kingdom. People were rushing everywhere, in groups, or one by one: black clad attendants, squires in bright colours, and many others from the town and from the country wide about. Many had been coming to the city since news of the king's death, seeking aid and bringing tidings from all corners of the country.

Flora and Simon nodded to Lavinia, the Lady of the Stag, who strode past them in the hall in her full armour, antlers rising into the air from her helmet. Since she'd helped lead the rebellion against the King Selenus, she had been advising Selena and was often somewhere close by.

When Simon opened the main door to the comfortable and large set of chambers he was sharing with the others, Anna came bounding across to him and grabbed him by the waist. She'd hardly been able to leave his side since they'd been reunited, and it was only with great reluctance that she let Simon train without her.

Johnny, Flora's older brother, who'd also been taken by the king, was sitting by the window, looking out over the square, holding his arms tightly around his chest. He turned, his face hollow and thin, and smiled weakly.

'What's up, Johnny?' said Flora in the American accent she sometimes used with him.

'Nuttin,' Johnny replied in the same tone, and Flora went over to join him, scrambling up and pointing out of the window down below at a group of squires playing a ball game. Johnny put his forehead against the window, and Flora placed an arm around his shoulders.

Simon tried to disentangle Anna from his waist. 'Can't I train with you?' she asked.

'No! How many times do I have to say it? No, you can't. It's far too dangerous, and you're –'

'Too young. Humph,' she said, and released Simon, folded her arms, and went back to her bed where she picked up a rag doll and started to play with its hair. 'Wasn't too young to get stolen away,' she said to the doll in an undertone just loud enough for Simon to hear.

Ignoring her, Simon went behind a wooden screen and undressed, washing himself in warm water scented with sweet herbs, then put on the clothes that Selena had given him.

Anna laughed when he came out. 'You look like a girl!'

'I do not,' he said hotly, and looked down at the long, gently shimmering gold and green robe. It billowed as he walked, and he hated it. But his own clothes – the jeans, the jumper, the T-shirt – had been taken away to be cleaned, and had not yet reappeared. His hair was getting longer too, something which he quite liked. He blew it away from his forehead, and he threw himself on to the soft bed.

None of them could really settle, and they played a game of catch with a rubber ball until the silver sun reached the high-point of the sky, and Johnny noted it was time to go.

They left Anna sulking by herself. 'Too young,' she muttered, and whispered to her doll. The doll, minding its own business, remained blank-faced, and Anna threw it to the other side of the room.

The Central Chamber was busy when the three friends arrived. Lavinia was deep in conversation with the young Knight of the Hawk. The whole company of the leading knights was there, some in armour, some in long robes like Simon's. The townspeople's representatives also thronged the room, dressed more soberly in blacks and greys.

A large, dark-skinned lady, wearing the rich silk robes of a knight, made way for Simon, Flora and Johnny as they entered. 'Thank you,' she said, her whole face beaming. 'You freed us from tyranny!' She took their hands and kissed them.

Each of the friends felt a blush rising. 'It was Andaria, really,' said Simon.

'But it was because of you!' answered the lady,

pressing his arm. He released himself with difficulty, and they hurried to their seats as the lady blew kisses after them. Another tried to stop them as they made for the table, but they squeezed past when Selena noticed them and motioned them through.

The Central Chamber was a large room with tall glass windows that looked out over the square below. Selena was sitting at the middle of the table, in a large wooden chair, and Simon squashed in at one end on a bench, in between Johnny and Flora.

Mithras, the demi-god of the Golden Realm, sat opposite Selena, arms folded calmly, and his supporters Cautes and Cautopates were on either side of him, their blond hair tinged by the sun pouring through the clear windows. Tall golden jugs filled with fragrant cordials, finely worked glasses, and plates of delicious-looking confections were laid along the table.

'Cautes.' Simon nodded to the man on Mithras's right. Cautes shook his head from side to side in response, flopping his hair over his forehead, and made a face at Simon that nobody else could see, sticking the tip of his tongue out and stretching his eyes, then popping a whole sweet in his mouth and gulping. Simon couldn't help but stifle a giggle. He was glad Cautes was going to come with them on their mission to the Centre of the Worlds.

They knew that Selenus had harmed the Threefold Goddess with his trap and set the worlds out of joint in doing so; they had to find out what he'd done, and stop it, or they would be trapped in the Silver Kingdom for the rest of their lives.

Their companion Pike, newly given his father's title of the Knight of the Shark, was standing behind the Lady of the Stag, and Simon caught his eye. He couldn't help winking, and Pike blushed. Pike's mother, the Lady of the Snake, was not there, but many others thronged around.

'Let us begin.' Selena banged the table and everyone fell silent. 'The messages, do you please.'

Lavinia rose. She was holding a bag of little packets, and unfolded each one carefully. 'Magehawks are coming in from all over the kingdom,' she said. 'They're bringing strange news. Forests withering, although it is summer; unknown beasts prowling; prodigies in the sky that no one can interpret; shadows forming in the far reaches of the kingdom . . .'

Concerned voices began to murmur.

'What about the other worlds? Did anyone try

to get through to the other worlds using their animals?' asked someone.

'The Knight of the Hawk – he has the talent. What do you say?' called Selena.

The Knight of the Hawk stood up. He was young, and his handsome face reddened. 'My queen . . . I tried . . . I could not contact my hawks. Something I cannot reach through blocks me. It pushes me back. It hurts, though I would try again if you wish.'

'I thank you, Knight of the Hawk,' said Selena. 'Do you please try again when you are rested.'

He nodded briefly, and ran his fingers through his thick brown hair before sitting down quickly.

The councillors were now all talking at once, each trying to get heard. All the voices were blurring into one. Everyone was getting up and sitting down, and sending messages by magehawks, and Queen Selena was watching and listening, her hand under her chin, paying careful attention and looking, despite her youthful age, regal.

Simon was feeling more and more annoyed. Nobody was doing anything useful. He wanted to get on and go to the Centre of the Worlds, and all they were doing was chattering. He coughed, but nobody listened; they all jabbered over him. He felt so helpless and ignored that, without thinking about what he was doing, he banged hard on the table and stood up, his chair legs scraping on the floor.

Everyone went silent. Flora tugged at his elbow, but he didn't sit down. 'Look,' said Simon. 'Flora and I have been stuck here four whole days now, ever since the king died, and what have you all been doing? *Talking.*' He hit his palm down on the table again, causing a glass to jump and clatter.

'Simon, do you please seat yourself,' said Queen Selena gently.

'You said we would go to the Centre of the Worlds,' said Simon, sitting down reluctantly. Flora grabbed his arm, as if to stop him in case he thought about getting up like that again. 'To find out why the Way is closed, what Selenus has done to damage it.'

'And you will,' Mithras interrupted. 'There is more than one difficulty, however. We have been trying to reach the priests at the Temple of the Threefold Goddess – the order went out for all priests to return to their temples after Selenus died. They will best advise us. Our magehawks do not return with any word from them. We sent the Lady of the Snake, but it is four days' ride, and it will be another four at least before she returns with any news.'

'Why do we need these priests?' asked Flora.

'Because they hold the key to the Centre,' replied Mithras quietly. 'And if they are not answering by magehawk, then there is only one thing to do. We shall have to go ourselves to see them.'

'Then let's go now,' said Simon. 'We'll catch up with the Lady of the Snake, or meet her coming back. I can't stand all this waiting about. I need to know – I *want* to know what's happening . . .' He tailed off, unable to complete the sentence that had formed in his mind.

'What's happening there?' came Johnny's sleepy, quiet voice. He'd picked up on Simon's tone. 'Back home, I mean. On planet Earth, the solar system, the Milky Way, etc. etc. We all want to know what's happening at home.'

'No one can see,' said Mithras. 'As the Knight of the Hawk says, there is something in the way, some veil, or wall even.'

'And what about the place where you put my parents?' asked Simon, suddenly anxious. The Golden Messengers had secreted them in a holding place between worlds, safe and out of the way, and he wondered if that had been affected.

'We cannot communicate with the Golden

Realm, so I cannot tell you if it still holds,' Mithras answered.

'Are they in danger?' asked Simon.

Mithras paused, and when he spoke there was a tightness in his voice. 'We are all in danger.'

'So let's go now!' said Simon. 'We're ready, we can deal with it.'

The councillors were murmuring among themselves, some impressed at his bravery, others thinking him rash.

'We need to discuss many things,' Lavinia cut in. 'Your training is hardly sufficient . . .'

Selena looked up. 'That is true.'

'We can fight!' said Simon. 'We got here on our own, and we've been learning from you . . .'

Frowning, Selena thought. 'It is a difficult journey. For now . . .' She paused, looking carefully at Simon and Flora, then placed her hands face down on the table. '. . . I forbid it.'

'That's it?' exploded Simon. 'We just have to wait here?'

'We must wait, at least until the time has passed for the Lady of the Snake to return. And till we leave, you and Flora and Johnny will continue to train.'

'But –' said Simon, deflated.

'The decision of the queen is final,' said Selena. 'We will wait until we hear from the Lady of the Snake.'

Simon kicked the back of the table leg in frustration as the discussion moved to the knights still loyal to the old king, Selenus, who were causing trouble in the city, led by Sir Ursus, Knight of the Black Lion.

The meeting went on, and Simon let his mind drift away from what they were saying. He sipped a cool, fresh cordial, and his eyelids began to droop.

It was Flora who noticed. She, too, had not been paying attention to the conversation, and had been looking out of the window.

'What's that?' She pointed out across the square.

Selena's voice faltered as the light in the room began to darken and shadows lengthened. Simon stood up, and saw in the distant sky a huge black mass covering the sun.

It was moving, and it was coming straight for the palace.

Simon ran to the window, and he was swiftly followed by everybody else, all calling and shouting.

'What is that?' said Flora, aghast.

They could answer the question soon enough.

'Magehawks,' said Pike, as the cloud got closer. 'Hundreds of them. Why aren't they travelling by the shadows?'

The enormous flock reached the square. But instead of settling, they continued to beat their wings.

And then they started to fling themselves at the glass of the windows of the Central Chamber.

One or two, stunned by the blow, fell to the square below, but where they fell, the others continued. A crack appeared in the glass. 'They're trying to get in!' shouted someone.

Simon, face right up to the window, met the staring white eyes of hundreds of magehawks. 'They've gone crazy,' he exclaimed.

'Out! Everybody out!' ordered Selena. There was a rush for the door. Flora leaped over a fallen chair, and Johnny slid round it, but Simon stumbled, and caught his foot. Birds' beaks tapped on the window.

'Come on, Simon!' yelled Flora.

Simon extricated himself and ran for the door, through which everyone else was already streaming.

As he reached it he couldn't help but look back towards the window.

The crack was getting wider and wider, smaller fissures spilling from it, like ripples in a lake. The mass of birds was breaking through.

Johnny grabbed Simon by the shoulders, but he resisted, wanting to see.

And as Johnny managed to pull him through the door, the glass gave way, shattering in a huge rush of air that blew through the room. Glass splintered everywhere, and the maddened, shrieking birds stormed in.

Johnny slammed the door shut on a magehawk's beak, and they stood with their backs to it, listening to the thumps of the birds hurling themselves against it.

'The door will hold,' said someone.

'There's a squire from the square . . . He's coming up . . .' said another.

Simon led the way into the main hall of the palace to meet the squire, who was loping in through the great doors, bedraggled and shocked.

'They're from the Borean priests,' he cried out, holding handfuls of paper. 'Raining down from the magehawks. It's mostly nonsense – just scribbles and symbols! But there are some phrases that keep repeating . . .'

'What are they? What do they say?' demanded Selena.

Outside, Simon could see many birds dropping to the ground, falling in piles, though with exhaustion or death he could not tell.

The squire paled as he read out the message, his voice trembling. '*Help! Bring help now!*' He paused, and glanced at Selena nervously.

'Go on! Read it!' Selena commanded.

The squire continued. '*Or everything will die.*'

Chapter Two

CONCERNING
CYGNET

'SIMON? SIMON? Can I go with you to the temple? Please?' Anna was dancing around Simon's legs and generally getting in the way as he hefted his belongings on to the horned horse he'd been assigned for the journey to the Temple of the Threefold Goddess: a mid-sized roan with short, pearly horns and a gentle gleam in his eyes.

The arrival of the magehawks and their message had changed Selena's mind, and she'd decided to go to the Temple of the Threefold Goddess herself to find out what was amiss there. *Everything will die.* It was too urgent to ignore. They were all getting ready, but Anna was to be left behind for her own safety.

Simon started putting things into saddlebags, occasionally stopping to pat or stroke the horse, and all the time trying to ignore Anna. He'd found his old clothes, fresh and clean, and had put them back on, stowing some spares of the Silver Kingdom in his bag.

The band of travellers was in the square outside the palace gates, loading up the horned horses with enough provisions to last the journey to the Temple of the Threefold Goddess – and back again, just in case. Each of them had been given a sword, a dagger, a bow and quiver of arrows, and a small shield that could be strapped on their backs.

It was the midpoint of the morning, the day after the magehawks had come, and the whole city was washed in silver light, glittering and fresh. The black glass towers, piercing the sky, shone. Bells tolled into the air, sweet and clear. All the pictures of Selenus had been torn down, and now that his presence was fully removed, the city felt as if it had struggled out from under a yoke.

Many palace servants were clearing away the dead magehawks and tending to those that were still alive.

Flora, who was wearing her old dress and filling up some saddlebags on her own horse with dried fruits, whistled, and Johnny caught the tune as he helped pack. It was something from their early childhood, a cartoon they'd always watched about Robin Hood, and before they finished it, they fell on each other, laughing.

Simon turned to his little sister who was now pulling at his sleeve. She was so small, so fragile, and his heart filled with love for her. 'There's nothing I can do,' he said as she asked him once more. 'You have to stay here. Don't worry, I'll be back soon, I promise.'

Anna left him, and appealed to Selena. The queen was checking over her huge, sable, horned horse, and tilted her head as she bent to look at its hooves. She was not yet used to the horns that had grown when she became queen, and could feel them weighing down on her. Standing up once more, she pulled up her specially made travelling hood, hiding them.

'Can I go?' asked Anna.

Selena shook her head firmly. 'We don't know what is happening up there. The magehawks were behaving so bizarrely . . . I've never seen anything like it. The Temple of the Threefold Goddess has always been a place of peace. It's hard to believe anything *so* wrong is happening.'

Anna twisted the folds of her dress in her hands, and looked up at Simon expectantly.

Simon guessed that she didn't want to be left with nobody she knew, among these strange black towers and the pale, armoured knights.

'You're too small for a horse, anyway,' said Selena, hoping that would clinch the matter.

'I can ride ponies! I won a competition.' Anna stopped, remembering the blue rosette that was pinned to the corkboard in her bedroom, at home in Limerton by the sea.

Selena smiled at Anna. 'You are brave, Anna. But you cannot come.'

They continued preparing the horses, and Simon forgot about Anna for a while as Lavinia took him, Flora and Johnny aside and put them through their sword paces. They practised for a while, parrying, thrusting, jumping, until Selena gave the sign for them all to get ready to mount.

Simon pulled at the hunting horn, which hung constantly at his side. Since the king had died it had been quiet, as if it were sleeping, though Simon knew how deadly its note could be. He saw

Flora's sunsword was in its sheath, hanging from her belt.

At last they were ready. Selena had given her final orders to the Knight of the Hawk and the Lady of the Stag, who were to rule the Council of the Silver Kingdom until Selena returned, communicating with her by magehawk. Mithras had vanished; they assumed that he would come and meet them by the city gates. Simon said goodbye to Anna, and left her in the care of the Lady of the Stag. He turned to wave, and saw that she had already begun chattering to her protector. Feeling that there was no need to worry about her, he joined Flora.

They crossed through the city streets quietly; there seemed to be no one about. Pike, in light armour, was on the lead horse; behind him came Cautes, who rode bareback on a grey with confidence and poise. Flora and Simon went abreast – Flora with ease, Simon a little less so, but enjoying the rhythm of the ride. Johnny and Selena took up the rear of the procession.

As they passed through the huge city gates set into the turreted walls that surrounded the capital, the royal guards raised their trumpets and blew a salute. The chief guard cried out, 'We wish you well. You have delivered us once; may you deliver us again.'

And then the whole wall came alive, the battlements thronged with people, all waving and cheering. Simon spotted Cautopates, who threw flowers down to them. Simon caught one, and handed it to Flora. It was blue, unlike any he'd seen before, with huge petals and a heady, delicious scent. Flora put it behind her ear.

'I *am* named after the goddess of flowers, after all,' she said.

They turned, waved and held their weapons in the air; then, borne on the tide of excitement, took the road in the direction of Boreas, the north wind, and the Temple of the Threefold Goddess.

As they were leaving the city, Simon was surprised to hear a voice he knew well.

'Wait! Wait!'

Hardly believing it, he looked over his shoulder to see Mithras approaching on a horse. He was about to relax, when he heard the voice again, crying for them to wait, and a head peeped out from behind Mithras.

Anna was sitting behind him, carrying a little

bag. Out of the top of the bag peered the head of her rag doll. Behind them came Selena's attendant, Clara, leading a small but sturdy pony.

The travellers drew to a halt. 'What's this?' said Selena lightly. 'Insurrection?'

Mithras, looking grave but with a glint in his eye, said, 'I guarantee the safety of this young lady.'

'It was my order that she does not come,' said Selena.

'Upon my honour,' said Mithras, 'she will be safe.'

He put Anna down gently on to the ground, and drew his horse towards Selena, where he whispered something in her ear. Meanwhile Anna let out a cry of excitement and began to jump up and down.

When Mithras had finished, Selena looked thoughtful. 'Anna,' said Selena quietly, calling Simon's sister to her. Anna, awed by Selena's bearing and her horns, came gently. Selena was holding something, which she revealed to Anna.

'This is a short dagger,' she said. 'I had it when I was your age.' Her voice wavered, and she paused a second before recovering. 'My father gave it to me. Look – see how its hilt is set with emeralds, and see the symbol of the moon on the dagger? It is a royal dagger, and its aim is true.' She slipped a little belt around Anna's waist, and placed the dagger in its sheath on the belt.

'Have you got one for my doll?' said Anna, and Selena laughed. 'She needs to be able to defend herself too!'

Selena's attendant, Clara, ran forwards. 'Will you give this fine young lady a weapon for her doll?' asked Selena.

Clara pulled a long pin from her hair, and gave it to Selena, who presented it courteously to Anna. Anna bobbed a little curtsey.

'Where did she learn how to do that?' whispered Flora to Simon, who shrugged in reply.

'The demi-god Mithras will protect Anna,' said Selena. 'Do you, Simon, object?'

Mithras had saved them before; Simon knew his power. If he was going to look after her, then it would be all right. Even before he could say anything, Anna mounted her little pony, reverently attached the hair-pin to the doll's skirts, and rode up to join Simon. 'See?' she said. 'I am coming after all.' And on she trotted, gabbling happily away to Selena.

One person in the city was not watching on the walls, and he was certainly not rejoicing. As the populace slowly returned to their homes and tasks, a slim, pale fifteen-year-old boy came quietly out of the side gates, cloaked up and muffled. He was riding a horned horse that looked well-fed and rested, carrying four large wicker panniers.

The boy was clutching a white swan's feather, and he brought it to his lips, and kissed it.

One of the panniers moved, and the lid poked up; inside was a hideous, little monkey-like face, looking out at him and grinning. Cygnet, only son of the Knight of the Swan, placed the swan's feather in a pouch around his neck, then threw the little creature a nut. Another pannier immediately opened up, revealing the creature's companion; it reached out and grabbed the nut from the other, and the two set up a furious chattering.

'Silence, beasts,' said Cygnet, and threw the second creature a nut as well. 'You will get a better reward soon enough.'

He set his horse in the direction of Boreas, chewed on a nut himself and spat out the husk, whilst the two little monkey creatures muttered and giggled. *I'll keep an hour behind the queen,* he thought. *They will not imagine they can be followed. They do not even know that I am alive.*

Although he had seen his father, the Knight of the Swan, kill himself when the king had died, in his mind he'd twisted the facts and they had become blurred and muddled. The rage he felt was everything, filling him like a stone.

He shifted his sword-belt around his waist, and trotted on.

'Those two killed my father,' said Cygnet quietly. 'Simon Goldhawk and Flora Williamson. And I am going to see that they pay for it.'

Chapter Three

The
Bound Mare

PIKE TURNED TO look at the city behind him as it shrank smaller and smaller in the distance. Since the king had died, sometimes the cruel face of the Knight of the Swan would appear in Pike's dreams; sometimes he would see the horrors of his father's Taking Apart.

Sometimes strange images from Earth flashed through his mind: the tent where he'd first met Simon and Flora; the place underground where they'd played that music – a nightclub, they'd called it . . . It all seemed so long ago since he'd fulfilled his mission to Selena and helped them come to the Silver Kingdom.

He was Knight of the Shark now, and he would have to do his father's memory honour.

He became lost in his thoughts as they went on.

The countryside to the Borean side of the city was scrubbier, and there were shrubs that lined the side of the road, their dark leaves threatening and warning.

Their riding formation had broken up already. Cautes was now up ahead, laughing with Johnny, tossing his blond hair and waving his arm expansively whilst Johnny listened intently. Anna was trotting along beside Selena, who was pointing out the mountains ahead and naming them for her. Mithras, unusually silent, sat straight up on his horse like a soldier, his godly radiance dimmed under a thick cloak.

Simon looked at Pike, dressed as he was in his new armour, and was reminded of the Knight of the Swan. Falling back a little, he felt in the bag attached to the left side of his saddle. In it was the locket he'd taken from the Knight of the Swan's body. Holding the reins of the horned horse with one hand, he managed to flick open the locket, and look at the lock of hair held within it. *Somebody loved you, once*, he thought.

Pensively, he gazed over his shoulder at the city.

'What's the matter?' asked Flora, turning her horse to come and ride beside him.

'Nothing,' said Simon. 'I just feel restless. Like something's not quite right.'

'Your face isn't quite right,' said Anna, falling back and catching the last bit of conversation.

'How we love our siblings,' Flora said to Simon in an undertone, grinning.

Simon arched his eyebrows in reply, and reached out to ruffle Anna's hair, causing her to trot away from him, sticking her tongue out.

After taking one last look at the city, Simon turned to face the mountains. The breeze was blowing from the north, and he felt as if it was calling him onwards.

When the silver sun was dipping below the white peaks, casting a dimmer glow across the plains and stretching the shadows of the mountains towards the wearying travellers, Selena called a halt. It was time to make camp. A day's journey, and as yet they had seen no signs of anything strange. Mithras, looking about, said that there was no need to worry, and here was as safe enough a place as any.

They dismounted, fed and watered the horned

horses, and tied them to trees. Cautes and Johnny started unpacking the bundles of tents, Anna dancing around them. Selena and Mithras were looking out towards the mountains, deep in conversation.

'Come on, Flors,' said Simon, catching her eye. 'Let's get some firewood.'

Flora followed Simon to where he was standing on the edge of the forest.

'You're just doing it to get out of putting up the tents,' said Flora when she reached him, and Simon shrugged.

'Maybe . . .' he replied.

'Here, take this lamp.' She offered one to him, along with a sparkstone, taking one for herself.

It was getting cold as they headed into the forest, and Simon drew together the folds of his thick grey cloak.

They came to a fork in the path and decided to split up, thinking it would be sensible to cover more ground between them.

Simon paused where the path branched, and made a mark with the tip of his dagger on one of the trees – an arrow, pointing back to the camp – and set off down the left-hand way.

He wasn't afraid, though twilight was approaching

and the forest was dark and full of whispering sounds. As he walked, he marked every ten trees, stooping to pick up branches until he had enough to make a good, thick bundle, which he tied round with a piece of rope, knotted, and hefted on to his back.

The air was darkening. He paused, breathing in the cool evening and listening to the noises of the forest. He fumbled with the sparkstone, managing to light the lamp after a few false starts. The glow it spread upon the forest floor was warm and bright, but the darkness outside the ring became even deeper.

Simon told himself to stay calm, and set off in the direction he'd come from, wood on his back, lamp in his hand.

He trudged along, his hearing heightened. The undergrowth was crackling with noise. He quickened his pace, feeling leaves crunch under his feet.

He'd been walking for a while when he realised that he hadn't counted the fourth mark back. Cursing silently, he stopped, and cast round with the lamp.

The sun had now set, and the reddish moon was only a little way up the sky. The stars, though bright, did not help, with their strange patterns. *If I was home, I could at least work out which way north is,* he thought.

Trying to remember what he'd seen as he started out, he moved on. That tree – its shape looked familiar, didn't it? It was tall and witchy, its branches spreading out towards him. He called out Flora's name, and listened hard for an answer.

None came. Only the breeze, and with it the groanings and grumblings and creakings of the forest.

About ten minutes later Simon stopped and realised he was lost. A little flicker of panic shivered through his body.

It's all right, he told himself. *The camp's just round the corner.*

Then why, came another voice in his head, *have I not seen a fire, heard voices?*

He tripped, dropping his bundle of wood, and held tightly to the lamp. It had a lot of oil in it; perhaps the best thing to do would be to find a place to wait out the night. He would be vulnerable and alone, but at least he had his dagger.

Something growled behind him, and he jumped, a shudder running through his entire body. He gulped, imagining ravening jaws, and shone his lamp on the place from where the sound came.

Whatever it was, though, must have skittered away; he heard the rustling in the bushes growing fainter, and in the silence that followed the growl did not return.

Ahead, something was glimmering through the branches. A light, but only a small one. *Maybe they put the fire out, and left the embers to guide me?* he thought, beginning to feel relieved. He half ran towards it.

Simon was about to call out in greeting when he noticed that the light was white and bright and steady. It was definitely not coming from a fire. Nor was it a lamp or a burning torch. He pushed on further, brushing aside low branches and tripping over roots, and then stopped in amazement.

The light was emanating from an animal that was standing in the middle of the path in front of him.

It was a horse.

Not a horned horse, like the ones in the Silver Kingdom, but a normal one, like those he knew from home. He could tell it was a mare, a grey one.

She was beautiful, and glowing with a silvery

light. Simon felt a rush of energy trembling through him.

The mare looked ill. Her coat was patchy and she was skinny. She shifted, as if she were in pain.

Simon said gently, almost to himself, 'What's wrong with you?'

The mare flared her nostrils and tried to shy away, but could not, as if restrained.

He moved closer, and saw a thin rope over the mare's muzzle that was also biting into her flanks. The rope went down her neck, and round her body, holding her front two legs together.

'You're trapped!' said Simon, reaching out to comfort her. 'Who did this to you?'

The rope tightened as his hand neared, causing the mare to whinny, bloodshot eyeballs rolling. She jerked her head away.

Appalled, Simon tried to pick up the rope. It slipped out of his fingers. The mare snorted feverishly and kicked with her back hooves.

'I'll get you out of this,' said Simon, reaching for his dagger. He grabbed hold of the rope where it weaved down her neck, and tried to cut it in two, setting to it with vigour.

But the rope was too tough, despite the sharpness

of the knife. Simon tried to manoeuvre the blade, carefully, fearful of hurting the mare more, and twisted his hand around the rope for a better cut.

He gasped. His hand felt like it had been burned, and worse, the rope had attached itself to his skin. When he tried to brush it off with his left hand, it stuck to that as well, binding his wrists like poisonous manacles.

Now he was joined to the mare, so close to her he could smell her steaming sweat.

And there was something else, too – a voice, ageless and vast, that spoke from the beginning and the end of time, echoing in his mind, but he could not make out the words.

He closed his eyes.

Then a vision came to him. He saw a blackness, apparently empty. And then, through the void, appeared first a silver sphere, then one of gold, then one of blue.

A woman rose from the void, tall, beautiful. Pierced by a ray of light, she split into three forms.

Simon understood that these three women were still part of one whole. The women danced together, and a snake was born from the dancing. The snake grew and grew and it turned into a shadow and the shadow lengthened and became the shadow of a man, a man with horns on his head, a pale face with reddened eyes and a wide grin.

Simon's eyes snapped open in shock, but the shadow was still there, now stretching along the path towards him. The rope burned his skin and the mare screamed and reared on to her hind legs.

The scream became a woman's and suddenly the mare was a woman, tall and graceful, with a long mane of hair, and there was such beauty and pain in her eyes; then her nose lengthened, the hair drew in, her shoulders bunched up and her arms elongated and she crouched on to the ground and she was a horse again. She bowed her head and collapsed, drawing Simon with her. He knew that he would be woven into her bonds, that he would be trapped with her, perhaps for eternity.

From the edges of his consciousness he perceived a rush of golden light that pushed itself into the shadow and edged it back. Simon felt the rope sliding down, leaving his skin with a terrible burn. The shadow sped away, and vanished.

Simon turned, gasping with shock, and saw Mithras, uncloaked – a glow coming from him that lit up the whole forest around them.

'Simon!' Mithras ran to him, took him by the arm. 'We were worried. You've been gone for half the night.'

'Half the night? I thought it was only an hour or so . . . Anyway, look! The mare!' He pointed, but there was nothing there.

'Let's get you to sleep,' said Mithras, and led Simon back to the camp, a powerful arm protectively over him.

Flora was waiting for him, wild-eyed, and Anna grabbed him, sobbing. Pike gave him a hot, spiced drink.

'The mare,' said Simon again, but nobody listened to him. The drink began to soothe him, and soon he was flat on his back, asleep, and nothing stirred in the campsite except those who watched as the red moon gently sank to the horizon.

Chapter Four

THE LADY
OF THE PASS

'SO WHAT IS the Golden Realm like?' Johnny was asking Cautes. The two of them were riding close to each other the next day.

Cautes laughed, leaned in towards him and said, 'I wish you could see it, Johnny. There's the wonder of the City of the Sun – where buildings glow like the stars . . . and the White Sea, where shining fish fly over the waves like jewels . . .'

Flora, who was on her horned horse just to the left of Johnny, fell back, feeling surprisingly jealous. She joined Simon and Pike, who were riding in silence together.

'Looks like it's us three again,' she said cheerily.

They'd been travelling for a while since the silver sun had risen, going steadily further northwards. The long black road that led from the Port of Notus in the south to the Temple of the Threefold Goddess in the north was now little more than a dirt track, although still wide enough for four horses to ride abreast. Sometimes they'd spy a farmhouse over the fields, and earlier in the day they'd crossed through a small village surrounding seven standing stones, but they hadn't seen any signs of people around.

Except for one old man, sitting by the wayside. He looked hungry, so they shared some bread with him, and gave him some of the spiced wine that Mithras and Cautes liked to drink. He took a long pull, and smacked his lips.

'You look like you're from the city. What news? I seen magehawks flying about like nothing else. Rider came up here the other day, wouldn't stop to tell what business. No one been out to see me.' He spat and scratched at his beard.

'The king has fallen, and trouble stirs,' said Selena. 'We ride for the Temple of the Threefold Goddess for guidance.'

The old man eyed them warily. 'You be careful in those hills. I seen things . . . not natural.'

When pressed, he would not say more, and so they rode on.

'He just wants to scare us,' said Simon to Flora, trying to reassure her worried look.

She pulled her cloak tighter around her in reply.

It was colder now, and clouds scudded more frequently over the sun, though the mountains seemed as far away as ever.

The landscape was becoming hillier, and the road was narrowing. The horses were having to pick their way over rocks and scree, and the travellers rode two abreast as the road thinned. It became more difficult to see ahead, as the way looped and meandered onwards.

As they were at the road's narrowest point, an arrow came from above and stuck into the flank of Mithras's beautiful grey horned horse. The horse whinnied and reared; Mithras, with a supreme effort, controlled it. The others held tight to their reins. Simon gathered in Anna's pony to the side of his own horse.

Another arrow flew down, and this one struck into one of Simon's saddlebags.

'Group together!' called Selena. 'Bows out!'

'I can't see anyone!' answered Pike, an arrow already notched.

A scramble of rocks trickled down to meet them, and there was a great roar as a wave of armed people came running down from over the top of the hill beside them.

'We can't escape!' shouted Selena. 'We'll be picked off if we try. Face them here!'

Simon turned his horse to the attackers, and Flora did so too. Pike and Cautes were already shooting into the rushing horde, and Mithras had uncloaked himself, but as yet remained still.

The front attacker, a scarred, helmeted woman, reached the level ground and ran at Selena with sword upraised; Selena parried the blow from above.

'Come on!' called Simon. Flora and Simon galloped forwards, yelling as loudly as they could, leaving Anna with Mithras and Johnny.

They scattered the attackers, but Simon was hit on the back by a missile and fell off his horse. Flora quickly jumped down to help him. There were about ten attackers, and they clearly knew how to fight. Flora, without thinking, unsheathed the sunsword, held it above her head and yelled into the air. It glowed dimly.

The attackers stopped, and turned to face her.

'The sunsword!' shouted their leader. 'A great prize indeed! And wielded by someone who is unsure how to use it, it seems . . . Attack!'

Panicking, Flora flailed at one of the men, who was rushing at her with a fearsome howl. Something seemed to be wrong with the sunsword. It didn't feel as powerful as usual, its hum was quieter. She clashed swords with her foe; there was a metallic clang and a hissing. Her enemy yelped and dropped his sword – it had become too hot to touch. But it hadn't split as Flora had been expecting.

Anna was on her pony, her face scrunched up with worry. Mithras was next to her, ready to protect her, Johnny clutching the reins of his horse beside him, as Simon ran to join Selena, back to back with her, facing a ring of attackers.

'That's *the* hunting horn, isn't it?' said the leader, scarred face snarling as she threatened them. 'Who are you people? And what are you doing up here?'

'I'll blow it!' said Simon suddenly. Some of the attackers muttered. 'Everyone stay back. Let us go. You know what this is – the horn of Mithras! The king hid it! And it caused his death!'

The leader drew her breath in sharply. 'You killed my king?' And with renewed force she charged at Simon, and knocked the hunting horn from his hand. It spun away from him, its strap straining, and Simon all but fell.

Cautes was continuing to shoot his arrows, but in the melee it was difficult even for him to aim true. He almost hit Selena by accident, and brought his bow up. He too jumped off his horse, and ran in with his sword.

The ten attackers were gaining the upper hand. Simon was fighting as best as he could with the dagger, fending off blows left and right, but staggered under the fury of the attack and fell. Selena was in hand-to-hand combat with the leader, but gradually being backed into a corner. Pike was facing three axe-wielding men, while Flora was tugging at her enemy's sword as he pulled at the hilt.

'At my command,' shouted the leader, 'take them!'

The attackers readied themselves, swords and axes menacing; then Mithras, in his calm, grave, quiet voice said, 'Stop.' He began to glow gently with his divine radiance. His light washed over everything, gilding them; for a moment it was as if they were all statues, caught in their movements, shaped from gold.

The radiance ebbed away. In the second of silence after it had gone, Flora took the opportunity to join with Cautes, and Selena bounded to Simon's side and helped him up. One of the three axemen took Pike by the shoulders.

'You, sir,' said the leader to Mithras, 'are from the Golden Realm. What business do you have here?'

'Let us talk,' replied Mithras.

'We are sworn enemies of the Realm,' said the leader. 'I am Lucia, Lady of the Pass of Boreas. I have been guarding this road these score of years at the king's command. The winters have come and gone, but I have never failed in my duty. And your party tells me you killed my king? Then I will be happy to kill you!'

'Wait!' Selena's voice rang out clearly into the cooling air. 'You have no need to do so. You are loyal, and for that I admire you. But your orders are now revoked.'

'On whose authority?'

Selena drew herself up as tall as she could, and ripped the hood off her head. Lucia gasped when she saw the horns. Then she made a signal to her followers, who lowered their weapons warily.

'Your majesty,' said Lucia. 'The king is dead? And you are the queen?'

'We have much to tell you,' replied Selena.

'And I you.' She coughed heavily, and bowed. 'Where are you going?'

Selena and Mithras exchanged a glance. 'We are going to the Temple of the Threefold Goddess.'

'If it please you, come with us. The path you are taking leads to danger. We can show you a safer way.'

The little group remounted, panting, and drank heavily of the water and spiced wine they'd brought in their panniers. Anna, who had never seen a fight like that before, looked pale and worn, and Simon hugged her till she murmured she was fine.

When they had rested a little, they set off, Lucia and the queen in the lead, deep in conversation.

About half an hour later, and some way off the road to the north-east, they clambered up a rocky path towards a small black fort. Hewn out of stone, it squatted on top of the highest hill, separated from the road by a wide chasm. A drawbridge descended as they approached and hit the ground with a loud clunk.

A few chickens were scrabbling around in a corner of the courtyard. A small, ragged boy sat on a step and gawped at them. And there, raising the drawbridge behind them, was the old man they'd seen earlier.

'One of my spies,' said Lucia. 'Not as stupid as he looks. He told us you were coming so we ambushed you.'

With her helmet off, Lucia looked even more frightening. A long scar went from her lip to her right cheek, and she had lost part of one ear. They trooped after her inside the fort.

It was musty there, and Lucia's small band of followers were attacking a roasted carcass that Simon hoped was a sheep, and devouring it lustily. Mithras had put his hood back up, and was talking gently to Cautes, who looked worried. Pike was fiddling with his dagger, and Flora was holding Anna's hand. Johnny was pale and pacing up and down, scratching his arms and muttering slightly to himself. When Flora went up to him he pushed her away, and she returned to Anna's side, enveloping her in a hug.

'My queen . . .' said Lucia. 'I beg you, tell me what happened to your father. And why do you travel with his slayers?'

Selena's lips trembled a little. 'The king . . . was mad,' she said finally. 'And he has been deposed. His killer is not here.'

Lucia nodded slowly. 'I did fear his madness, my queen. We waited here for his orders, and some did come, but they were strange . . . Something has happened since. We felt it, five days hence. Something . . . breaking. And then, in the woods and the hills, we have seen odd things . . .'

'It was on that day he died. What have you seen?'

The followers went quiet. Lucia continued, 'Things decaying. And then there are the creatures – beings we have not seen before. We are frightened. I will admit that. We want to go home.'

'Will you lead us safely through to the Temple of the Threefold Goddess?' asked Selena.

'My queen, I have waited here, year after year. It is a long time since I sat in a comfortable chair in my tower in the city, with a glass of spiced wine and a hot scented bath ready for me, and the song of my heart's love in the next chamber . . .'

Selena put her hand to her chest. 'You have been

good servants of my father. I release you from your bonds. Put us on the safest path, and you may return home.'

Lucia's followers cheered, and Lucia herself placed her hand on her heart, and a single tear came down her cheek.

'Then please, my queen, take provisions from us if you need them, and I will set you on your way now.' She went to a table on which a map was laid. 'The road you were on would have taken you straight into the middle of the strangenesses. I saw a beast there – huge, its breath made everything dry and dead before it. You need to take this pathway,' she continued, tracing a line on the map, 'that skirts round the foothills to a pass through the mountains a little further in the direction of Boreas. It will take you from the rising of the sun till the middle of the day. And then once through the pass you journey towards Zephyr for one day, and you will reach the Temple to the Threefold Goddess soon after.'

'Have you had any contact with the Borean priests?' asked Selena.

'None,' replied Lucia. 'We saw a flock of magehawks, but we could not intercept them. There was also a rider galloping towards them the other day.'

Pike started. 'A rider? Did you see who it was?'

'The horse was moving too fast.'

'That must have been my mother, the Lady of the Snake . . .'

'Then I am afraid to tell you,' said Lucia, as gently as she could in her hoarse voice, 'that she took the main road . . . She may be dead by now.'

Pike's mind was a rushing of confusion and grief. 'It can't be . . . She's too strong, she'll find a way out . . . Mithras, she wouldn't die, would she? She's your companion, your helper, from the Golden Realm – you wouldn't let her!'

Mithras said simply, 'I cannot control all things, Knight of the Shark.' Cautes left Mithras's side and held Pike as he sobbed into his shoulder, and all were silent.

When he'd finished, he wiped his face with his arm, sniffed, and said, 'She isn't dead. I know it. I'd feel it if she was. I'd have . . . seen it somehow.'

'You may think what you wish, young knight,' said Lucia gruffly. 'Now. You had better make preparations to go.'

Chapter Five

THE
LONELY BEAST

THE MOOD WAS subdued as the companions left the stone fort behind. They'd not really rested, but had loaded up with extra provisions for the longer way round – newly made flat bread, fresh, smelly cheese, a couple of scraggly chickens, and more flagons of wine.

They watched Lucia and her somewhat bedraggled followers cheerfully march away in the direction of the city, and when they had disappeared, all they could hear was the distant boom of the magehawk entering the shadows, bringing news of Lucia's return to the capital city.

The sun's warmth was thin, and dark clouds swam around the edges of the sky. Even Anna, who had been so greatly excited by the whole expedition, was quiet and didn't let out a squeak during the long ride. The countryside was becoming hillier – dark green swathes of rolling slopes dotted with clumps of the black trees native to the Silver Kingdom.

Only Mithras remained serene. Everybody else was on alert; the slightest noise increased their jumpiness.

Cautes himself rode ahead with his bow at the ready, holding the reins lightly with one hand. Johnny, who'd taken a liking to Cautes, went with him. Having seen his sister Flora fight, he was confused within himself. He'd never held a sword before, still less killed anybody. It made him feel weak and stupid to be so useless, and being with Cautes lightened that a little.

Pike rode behind them, watching carefully, then Selena, followed by Flora and Simon, with Anna trotting along beside Simon. Mithras brought up the rear, hooded, cloaked, and calm.

They travelled at a steady pace. Simon liked the feel of the horse underneath him, and he stroked its little horns from time to time. The saddle was wide and made for long rides; although he was getting sore, he tried not to notice it, and instead breathed in the pure clean air.

The only life they saw was a bird, a raptor of some sort, which swooped and circled far above in search of something to hunt, and then it too vanished.

As twilight approached, they reached the foothills of the mountains, which rose up huge and imposing in front of them. The jagged summits were dusted with snow. Simon could see his breath on the air, and he shivered. His fingers were reddening and he blew on them to warm them up.

Mithras sniffed the air and looked about. 'It all feels safe,' he said. 'I sense no disturbances.'

Cautes got off his horse and pulled down a pallet of wood that Lucia had given them. As he did so he tilted his head sideways at Simon and Flora, and pretended that the pallet was too heavy for him, buckling and staggering like an old man. They couldn't help laughing.

Within ten minutes Cautes had a good fire blazing as they put up their tents in the shelter of a hill, protected from the snow-tinted Borean wind by a small ridge. Anna was huddled up in a bundle close to the flames, already asleep.

Pike pulled out a couple of dead chickens from his panniers, which they plucked and then roasted over the fire. They were thin, but Simon felt he'd never tasted anything so delicious. Cautes sucked daintily at a wing, whilst the rest of them guzzled – all except Mithras, who ate nothing, and Selena, who simply gazed into the fire.

After they'd finished there was silence, and then Mithras sang. His voice was gentle and warm, and his song was of the universe as it was when it began: the void, and the goddess, and the snake, and the three worlds of silver, gold and blue. The tune was sad and lilting, yet Simon went to sleep content. *My dream*, he thought. *I must ask Mithras about my dream of the mare.*

A fierce scrabbling noise woke Simon. He opened his eyes, and then gasped in fear. Framed in the light from the fire, and staring right at him, was the monkeyish, wizened face of one of King Selenus's pets. Simon yelled out a warning to the others, and the creature grinned, spat, and scampered away.

Simon scrambled outside and saw that Pike, who was keeping watch by the fire, was already chasing after it.

'Stop! It could be a trap!' called Simon.

'That hideous thing!' answered Pike, stopping and bending over, putting his hands on his knees and panting. 'It sneaked right up into the tents. I never saw it until it was running away. Is anyone hurt?'

By now everybody was awake and peering out from their tents. They gathered around the fire, which was low and only glowing with a few embers.

'It can't have been,' said Selena when they told her. 'I thought they'd been captured.'

'Apparently not,' said Pike.

'I will watch with Mithras for the rest of the night,' said Cautes. 'Then as soon as dawn comes, we will go through the pass.'

Simon slept after that, whilst Cautes and Mithras sat in silence, gazing at the stars, until the sky began to lighten.

Dawn came quickly in the Silver Kingdom, and the silver sun soon flooded the hills with its beams.

They set off with haste. Anna was swaddled up in furs; Flora had put on Johnny's leather jacket over her new clothes, and Simon had on his jumper from home as well as his cloak. Simply smelling it reminded him of his parents, and made him hope they were all right.

His horse took the steepening path easily, picking its way sure-footedly over the rocks. The sides of the mountains rose on either side of them, rocky and inhospitable. The pass cut straight through the mountain range and then brought them out on the other side on to a wide plain.

They had been travelling along it for about an hour, when they heard the first howl. Cautes immediately turned around on his horse, his blond hair flowing in the breeze.

'What is it?' said Simon, muffled through the thick scarf he'd wound round his neck.

'I've never heard that noise before. It doesn't sound like a wolf. Bears don't make that sound,' said Pike.

'I've never heard a bear,' said Flora lightly, 'so I wouldn't know.'

'Keep close, Anna,' said Simon, as Flora moved to her other side.

Mithras was looking keenly about. 'Something's wrong,' he said. 'There's something here that . . . shouldn't be here.'

The howl came again. It carried in it a weight of pain and frustration, sounding almost human. *Maybe it is*, thought Simon. There was something in that howl that made the back of Simon's neck bristle with fear.

'Keep going,' called Selena. 'Don't stop. We must make it to the end of the pass.'

They stepped up the pace. The horned horses were trotting now, with Anna's little pony stepping neatly alongside Simon. The mountains were sheer on either side; the path was just wide enough for three.

On they pressed. The wind was seeping through the gaps in Simon's clothes. His vision was hampered by the scarf, which he'd pulled right up to his eyes.

'Watch out for ice!' came Cautes's voice, as his horse slipped and almost fell. He managed to right it, and rode back to the others. 'It's not far now.'

The howl sounded once more, much nearer to them, somewhere up above and to the left of Simon.

'I don't like it!' said Anna indistinctly. She clutched her doll into the crook of her arm and felt for the handle of her dagger.

'Keep going!' called Cautes. They began to move faster towards the end of the pass. Their horses' breath made great clouds in the cold air. 'Keep in a straight line!' Cautes pulled up next to Anna. 'Anna, get on my horse.'

'But what about my pony?'

'He'll be lighter without you.' Cautes grabbed her by the shoulders and hefted her on to the saddle in front of him. 'Now let's go!'

There was a roar now, terrifying in its nearness. Though Simon knew it was impossible, he could not help but feel that he was rushing into the maw of some terrible beast.

Ice and scree fell around them. The ears on Simon's horned horse went backwards. *He's terrified*, thought Simon. And then, as if they were one being, all the horned horses started to gallop as fast as they could.

Simon leaned down as far as he could into his horned horse's mane, and held tightly to the reins. 'Get us out of here!' he whispered.

He couldn't see anything but snow and rock. He hoped the others were near him. All he could hear was the thundering of his own horned horse's hooves, and the roaring of the beast, which was now almost upon them.

A muffled scream burst from behind. Simon turned his head to the left and saw a commotion. Cautes's horse was coming towards him – but Cautes was not on it. Anna was clinging on to the horse's neck, and she was shrieking.

'He fell off!' she shouted.

'Help!' called Simon. 'Anyone!'

Nobody answered. They must have rushed on further. Glancing about furiously, he could see nothing except drifts of snow. With great difficulty he reined in his horse and reached out to catch Anna's as she went by. He managed to grab hold, though his own horse was jittery. 'Hold on, Anna,' he said. 'Head out of the pass, and wait by the entrance!'

She set off at a slower pace, and Simon turned his horse's head towards the noise. His horse whinnied. 'Come on! Cautes is there! He needs our help!'

He urged the horse back.

Simon saw through the gloom in front of him a vast grey shape, furred and tusked, with four legs, worrying at something. As he came nearer, the shape rose on to two legs and roared, its teeth sharp and gleaming. It threw itself down again on to something that, with a horrifying lurch in the pit of his stomach, Simon realised was Cautes.

He scrabbled for the hunting horn and put it to his frozen lips and blew. But the sound that came out was weak, and had no effect. He tried once more but what ensued was even weaker.

Nothing else for it, he thought. He whispered to his horse to stay, jumped down and took aim with his bow and arrow.

A scream from Cautes made him lose his grip. The arrow shot uselessly into the air.

Come on, he thought. Steadying himself, he sighted along the arrow and let go. He hit the beast with a satisfying thud, and it was maddened enough to rear up on to its back two legs again, by which time Simon had fitted another arrow to his bow and let loose. This time, the arrow buried itself into the beast's right flank. Roaring, the beast scanned the gloom for its attacker.

How many arrows does it take? thought Simon. *What* is *that thing?* He quickly felt in his quiver. Eight left.

Trembling, he notched another arrow as the beast started lumbering towards him.

Oh hell, he thought, and let loose blindly. The arrow buried into the beast's neck, but still it came onwards.

Simon gulped. He looked for his horse – but it was nowhere to be seen. Where was everyone? The beast was lumbering straight at him. He drew his sword, ready for one last defence. The beast's eyes were alien, unfeeling, and glared at him. *I am nothing to it*, he thought.

There was a whooshing sound, and an arrow flew over his head and into the chest of the beast. It was followed immediately by another. The arrow must have struck its heart, because this time the beast groaned in pain, and wavered on its giant legs. It moaned once more – a long, low moan – and clawed at the arrow, trying to pull it out. It collapsed on to four legs, and with its tusks tried to scratch at the places where it had been shot. Then its knees buckled, and it swayed from left to right before falling to the ground, exhaling long and loudly. Simon, panting, watched as life ebbed from the creature, until it was nothing but a hideous husk.

'Just in time,' panted a voice, and someone patted him on the shoulder. It was Flora. 'Got him, didn't I?' she said tautly.

Simon blurted out thanks, and the two briefly hugged. 'We've got to save Cautes!'

Edging past the massive carcass and trying not to look at it, they saw Cautes lying on the path. They ran to him and knelt down, and it was all both of them could do not to be sick.

Cautes looked like a puppet, limp and lifeless.

'Is he breathing?' asked Flora, ashen-faced.

Simon stroked the hair away from Cautes's neck, and felt for a pulse.

Cautes's eyelids fluttered, and he opened them.

'You're alive, Cautes!' shouted Flora.

'What happened? My . . . my leg!'

Simon looked down the length of Cautes's body. His right leg was so mangled that it had almost come off at the knee.

Chapter Six

THE TEMPLE OF THE THREEFOLD GODDESS

SIMON AND FLORA splinted and bandaged up the damaged Cautes as best as they could as he lay there in the snow.

Simon was almost gagging at the sight of the blood as they used his cloak as a tourniquet. Cautes screamed in pain, and seeing that friendly, witty face screwed up in agony was almost too much to bear.

Flora and Simon lifted him up together with a great effort and put him on Flora's horse, which they led towards the end of the pass. Simon wondered aloud if there were any more of those horrible creatures around. Nobody answered.

Cautes sat oddly, slumped forwards. After about ten minutes he raised himself a little and attempted a smile. 'That thing was ugly . . .' he said, although it came out as more of a gasp.

'Cautes! What happened?' It was Selena, riding towards them on her own horse, and leading Simon's. 'Where are the others?'

Flora and Simon got on to Simon's horse, and they moved onward as quickly as they could. There was no sign of anyone else, and Simon began to worry. Mithras had sworn he would protect Anna – but where was he?

'Not far now,' said Selena. The sides of the mountains were sloping more gently, and the ground was becoming patchy with the thick, blackish grass of the Silver Kingdom.

At last the pass opened out on to a broad, dark plain, spotted with copses of bare-looking trees. Underneath the nearest were two horses – and there was Mithras, with Anna clinging to him, and Pike and Johnny with arrows notched.

Mithras, looking concerned, immediately came to Cautes's side, leaving Anna with Pike and Johnny.

'Took a chunk out of me,' said Cautes glibly.

'Is there anything you can do?' Simon asked Mithras.

'My dear Cautes,' said Mithras, shaking his head, and he stood on his toes to kiss Cautes on the forehead. He must have delivered some healing energy, supposed Simon, as Cautes immediately brightened, and shrugged.

'I've never seen anything like it,' he said.

Mithras frowned. 'The king's trap has caused further disturbances – it seems as if that creature has wandered into this kingdom from another.'

'Not the Golden Realm, that's for sure,' said Cautes. 'You ever seen anything like that back at your place?'

Flora shook her head vehemently. 'No way. That was no bear. It had tusks! And those teeth . . . Plus it was huge. Like, *really* huge.'

'Then where did it come from?' mused Mithras.

'Wherever it's come from,' said Simon, 'it must have travelled here somehow . . . I remember the ambassadors from the Golden Realm saying they were looking at other ways of travelling between the worlds.'

'Dangerous ways,' said Mithras. 'Ways that upset the balance, as the king clearly has. When he set his trap to break the Way, other things must have got caught up in it.'

Like us, thought Simon.

'Let's get on,' said Selena. 'I grow more fearful by the minute.'

After feeding and watering the horses, then drinking some spiced wine and wolfing down some nuts and fruits, they set off.

Anna, riding closely next to Simon, said, 'I looked after myself. I came out on the horse all by myself and waited like you said till Mithras found me.'

'Well done,' said Simon. 'You stick close to him.'

'We can only go as fast as Cautes,' said Selena impatiently as Flora kicked her horse onwards. 'That means walking pace. You can't trot or canter, can you?' she asked Cautes.

Cautes winced a little. 'I can try.'

So they went on at a gentle trot. The way was clear of mist and snow. They could see to the north, east and west across the flat plain; behind them to the south, in the direction of the capital city and the Port of Notus, was the mountain range.

Simon thought of the beast, dying in a place it hadn't understood, unburied and unmourned.

* * *

That night they camped in the shelter of a clump of spiky black trees. Mithras kept watch, huddled in his cloak, whilst the others slept.

The night was clear and quiet, and they were disturbed by nothing. Still, Simon had not got used to the moon's red tinge, and he slept fitfully, slipping in and out of dreams.

The mare he'd seen, tied up and hurt – what had she been? Why had she appeared to him? As they neared the Temple of the Threefold Goddess, her form kept returning to his mind, and he felt a great weight upon him.

As they were setting off the next day, Simon rode up towards Mithras and asked him about the mare he'd seen in the forest.

'Troubling,' said Mithras. 'Yet more troubling things.' He turned his face away. 'I fear it was an emanation of the goddess – one of her three parts. She sometimes comes to us as a mare. I dream of her as an eagle. But what disturbs me further is that I have not seen her, even in my dreams, since I came to the Silver Kingdom.'

They travelled slowly for a while, trying to keep Cautes as comfortable as possible. Selena rode by his side, and pressed leather water pouches to his lips whenever he faltered. They stopped every now and again to make sure that the dressing on his leg was clean.

Selena was getting anxious. There could be any number of beasts like that, ravaging the kingdom, and they were no nearer to finding out how to stop it. As they were waiting whilst Mithras patiently washed Cautes's leg, a small shape came from a patch of shadow in the direction of Notus.

'A magehawk!' Anna, with her keen sight, spotted it first. 'I can see its white eyes!'

The magehawk, making its peculiar booming, its shadowy wings fluttering, flew down and settled on Selena's shoulder, dropping a small packet into her outstretched hands. She unfolded it, and her forehead creased.

'What's the matter?' asked Pike.

'Trouble in the city.' She frowned. 'Sir Ursus, Knight of the Black Lion, a supporter of my father, is trying to wrest power from the Lady of the Stag. She begs me to return.'

She stared into the distance. 'Your mission is too important. We are near the Temple of the Threefold Goddess. I will see you safely there, as I have promised, and into the hands of the priests in the knowledge that they will deliver you into the Centre of the Worlds. And then I will return.'

She scribbled on the back of the message, placed it in the magehawk's beak, whispered into its ear, and it flew back off into the shadows.

The path began to widen, now formed of well-cut, light-coloured paving stones, although there were cracks, and weeds pushed their way through the surface.

When they turned round a long bend and came upon the vista that led to the Temple of the Threefold Goddess, none of them could help stopping to take it in.

It was a tall, glass pyramid, pointing into the sky as if reaching up towards the heavens. On either side of it were two smaller glass pyramids. A stream came down from the hills above it, creating a waterfall that threw up spray so that the light refracted in the glass, making hundreds of tiny rainbows.

Around the base of the main pyramid were smaller buildings, all glass and pointed. The complex of buildings was like nothing Simon had ever seen before.

They rode along the path, which straightened and went up a little rise towards the outer stone buildings.

'Why is it so quiet?' said Pike warily.

Simon felt the silence, thick in the air. They moved quietly, carefully, each understanding that they ought not to make too much noise.

'I was expecting a welcome, at least,' said Selena as they passed the first of the low stone buildings. The door hung open; nothing stirred inside.

Anna clutched her doll tighter. 'Don't worry,' she whispered to it. 'I'll protect you.'

'We shall head to the main temple,' said Mithras, but Simon detected a note of uneasiness even in his voice.

They came to the base of the largest pyramid. Nothing moved: not a rat, nor a spider.

'I'll go first,' said Pike, eyeing the huge triangular door at the foot of the pyramid.

'I'll go with you,' said Simon.

Flora, not needing to say anything, simply got off her horse.

The three of them tethered their horses to a post.

'Look in,' said Mithras, 'and come straight out.'

Trying not to appear as if he was scared, Simon squared his shoulders. 'Right,' he said.

'Come on, Simon,' said Flora. 'We've faced worse.'

'OK,' said Simon. 'Let's do it.' He pushed gingerly

at the huge door, and it creaked open.

And through the portal of the temple they went.

Light washed through the glass sides of the pyramid. In front of them stretched a broad expanse of white marble, and at the other end of the pyramid was what looked like a large altar. The space was huge, echoing and empty.

'It's fine,' said Simon to the others. 'There's nobody here.'

They relaxed, and started to look more closely at what was around them. Simon noticed a beautiful golden miniature statue of a bird-deer. He moved towards it, and reached out to pick it up, turning round to the others at the same time. 'Hey!' he said. 'Look! It's like the golden messengers . . .' He closed his fingers over it.

And then something hurled itself at Simon. He couldn't see exactly what it was, but its face was covered in strange symbols, and it had three horns coming out of its forehead. A confused muffled sound was coming from it. It knocked him to the ground and gripped his head.

Simon tried to grapple with it as it yanked a clump of his hair, pulling it so tightly that it stung. 'Pike! Flora! Help!'

He tried to push it off, sensing some commotion around him, but he couldn't work out what was going on.

Then he realised that it was a sound he hadn't heard for some time.

Far from rushing to help him, Pike and Flora were laughing.

The hand stopped pulling his hair, and he was released.

He looked up to see a boy about ten years old sitting on his chest and pushing a mask back off his face. 'I thought you were robbers,' he said crossly.

'Who are you?' said Pike.

'Who am *I*?' said the boy. 'I might as well ask you the same question. Nobody's been up here for *so long*.'

'Why don't you tell us who you are?' said Pike.

The boy got off Simon, stood up as tall as he could, and said petulantly, 'I'm the last remaining priest of the Threefold Goddess, of course!'

Chapter Seven

THE
LAST PRIEST

THE LAST BOREAN priest of the Threefold Goddess looked as if he might be about to cry. His upper lip trembled and he threw his horned mask down on to the ground.

'A calamity!' Mithras whispered to Selena. 'He will not know the way to the Centre . . .' They were all in the pyramidal temple now, standing by the entrance. Cautes was on the floor, resting on cushions they'd found by the side, his mangled leg raised up off the ground.

Sun poured through the glass walls. Overgrown plants trailed their way out of pots; leaves and balls of dust were scattered everywhere.

A candle was burning on the altar, on which was an image of three interlocking circles. Picked out in mosaic and running round the altar was a frieze: bird-deer chased each other through the air, an eagle pounced, a horse raced; a whale swam gracefully through the oceans.

'You're only a little boy,' said Anna to the priest. She was cross-legged on the floor, her doll placed carefully at her feet.

'Tell us what happened,' asked Selena gently.

The boy priest sat down on the ground and wrapped his arms around his knees. It was all Flora could do not to rush over and hug him.

'I don't need looking after,' snapped the boy, sensing the concern in the air. He locked eyes on Anna. 'Why are you playing with a doll? Haven't you grown out of that yet?'

'She is not just a doll,' said Anna crossly. 'She's special. Selena gave her to me. Look!' She held up the doll. 'Can't you see?'

'Looks just like a stupid doll to me,' said the boy.

'She's not!' Anna answered shrilly.

'Now, now,' said Selena, slightly at a loss.

'Please, good priest, do you tell us what has happened here.'

The boy priest sighed, and glared at Anna. 'My name is Arion. My father was the head priest. Only he . . .' He paused, fiddling with the mask. 'He died.' Then, savagely to Anna, he added, 'I stopped playing with dolls years ago!'

'Shut up!' said Anna fiercely. She embraced the doll. 'I'll stick you with my dagger if you're not careful!' She showed him the jewelled hilt.

'Anna!' gasped Simon, shocked, and she pushed it back, sulkily.

'Silence!' Mithras's powerful voice rolled through the temple, seeming to bounce off the glass walls. Both Anna and Arion hung their heads, as if they'd just been told off.

Arion sniffed and wiped his nose. 'When the king ordered the closing of the temple, my father only pretended to leave. He came back secretly with me and kept up the worship of the goddess. All the other priests left, and I do not know where they have gone. And then one day my father fell, picking fruit from a tree, and when I came out he was just lying there . . . I couldn't move him at first, but I managed to drag him out to the ice room.'

'When was this?'

'I don't know. I lost track of the days. I tried counting but I got confused.'

'Then we shall give him due honour,' said Selena, 'as soon as we can.'

Arion smiled. 'I give you thanks,' he said.

'There is one thing we must know. Why did you send so many magehawks?' asked Selena.

'I was scared . . . alone. I kept them. They kept me company. But I felt something, a few days ago. A . . . breaking. And I saw *something* in my dreams. It said everything would die unless I sent to the city for help. I didn't know what it meant, but I thought I would try to find out what happened and sent the magehawks.'

'What did you see?' said Selena gently.

Arion screwed up his face. 'Something I didn't understand. An eagle – a talking eagle. I tried to send just one magehawk to the capital, but somehow I got everything wrong, and I made the working too strong and hundreds and hundreds of them arrived . . .'

'I see,' nodded Mithras. 'And you forgot to send them by the shadows.' The sunlight gleamed off his golden hair. He looked pensively into the distance.

Arion nodded.

Pike coughed, and, turning to Mithras, said, 'May I ask something?'

Mithras assented.

'I wondered if you had seen my mother? She is called Melissa, the Lady of the Snake. She was sent here to find out what was happening.'

Arion shook his head. 'Nobody else has come here.'

Pike looked away, and Flora squeezed his shoulder.

'Then let us honour your father,' said Mithras gently.

They left Cautes lying by the entrance in a patch of light, and Arion took them outside.

Leading their horned horses around the back of the main temple, they found a large stable, now empty. Although there was no clean hay, there was a small rivulet running down from the mountain, and the horned horses drank greedily before settling in their stalls.

Mithras spent a moment or two tending to his wounded beast, making sure that he was comfortable, before turning to join the others. Flora and Simon gathered some grasses and saw that the horned horses had enough to eat.

Arion then led them through a smaller door into a building attached to the back of the main glass pyramid. It was ordinary, low, made of stone, and dark. They walked in single file down a corridor, past what looked like the refectory and the storerooms, until they came out into the cool clear day to a small vegetable garden, in the centre of which was a stone structure with a narrow entrance.

This was the cold room, dug deep into the earth, where ice and meat used to be kept.

Arion looked at the ground. Mithras nodded and, followed by Pike and Selena, ducked down into the cold room.

A few minutes passed by. Anna went to sit by Arion, and offered him a piece of grass, which she then began twisting round his finger when he paid no attention. This made him smile a little, and soon he was doing the same to her.

Simon leaned against the wall, thinking about the mare that he'd seen in the woods, and the beast that lay dead in the snow, whilst Flora fiddled with the sunsword and Johnny sat by himself, twisting his hair around his finger.

Pike's back appeared in the gap, and soon the three reappeared, bearing between them a cloth-covered body.

It was the custom of the Borean priests to bury

their dead on the mountainside, so they carried him up behind the temple, and Arion chose a place near the waterfall.

They worked steadily, all of them helping to dig out the grave, hefting out the hard earth with spades. Sweat trickled down Simon's back, and Johnny's muscles showed in his thin arms. Pike worked diligently and deftly. Only Mithras showed no signs of wearying.

As the sun moved down the sky, they became one with the rhythm of the work; nobody spoke. There was no need.

When they had finished, they gently lowered Arion's father into the grave. Mithras moved to the head of the group to say the prayer of burial, but Arion said, 'My lord, I wish to do it. I am the only priest of Boreas now, and I must fulfil my duty.'

He bowed low to the north wind, and said a simple prayer. 'Boreas now scatters your soul to the stars.'

There was silence, then Arion dropped a scarlet flower on to his father's body. Flora added the blue flower she'd been given when they'd left the city. It was drooping, but its colour was still bright, and then they filled in the grave.

They returned to the inner temple in sombre mood. Arion quartered them in the priests' cells, which were in a stone back-building along a corridor – sparse rooms, though warmly bedded. 'We will talk in the morning,' he said, leaving them. 'I must watch this night.'

Simon lay on his narrow bed staring at the tiny window in the wall above him for a long time. He was so far from his room at home. He'd lost count of the days he'd been away and had no idea how much time had passed on Earth, or if it had even been passing at all.

He heard something scratching in the night, insistent and worrying. Soon the sound became too loud to ignore. After a while he couldn't stand it any longer and got out of bed, pulling on his jeans and jumper, then opened the door to the corridor.

The noise was coming from the main temple. Simon expected to see other doors opening, but none did. The crimson-tinted light of the moon was shining through the windows. Impelled, Simon walked towards the sound, entering the great glass hall of the pyramid.

It took him a moment to adjust his eyesight. Torches were flickering along the sides of the vast room, candlelight glinting off the glass and the ornamental bird-deer.

And in the centre was a shape, its outline unsettling. Simon wondered what was wrong with it, and then he realised.

It was a bird – large, larger than a child – and its wings were bound to its sides. It was squirming, its claws skittering uselessly from side to side.

Filled with pity, Simon went towards it, thinking he might be able to release it.

As he neared he realised it was an eagle, magnificent and wild, eyes gleaming, the universe in its gaze. Its beak was bound, too. Simon's heart was aching for it.

Simon was within a few paces of it when a small voice said, 'Don't.'

Arion appeared from out of the shadows.

'What have you done?' said Simon.

'It is not me,' said Arion. 'She appears like this, every night, for half an hour or so. It is really why I sent the magehawks, for it was her who told me to send for help. You cannot go near her. Try.'

Simon went forwards a step or two, and then was knocked back by a strong force, like a shove in the stomach.

They watched her, helplessly. Sometimes a hissing sound escaped from her beak, and the eagle shifted and flopped.

After what seemed like an unbearably long time, the eagle shivered, arched her neck, then vanished.

'What is it?' asked Simon.

'Look at the mosaics,' replied Arion, pointing to the altar. 'You see? The mare and the eagle. They are aspects of the Threefold Goddess. The first, and most important, is a woman. But the eagle is hobbled. How can this be?'

'And the mare!' said Simon, and he told Arion about what he had seen in the forest.

'Then two aspects of the goddess are in trouble,' Arion said, scratching his head. 'The mare and the eagle. The third, most powerful part, shown by the woman . . . I do not know what has happened to her. And it makes me frightened. I think that nothing can be healed until these parts are freed.'

'Do you pray to the goddess?' asked Simon.

'I do,' said the small priest. He said no more, and something about the set of his face suggested to Simon that though he prayed hard, the goddess did not give him the answers he wanted.

* * *

The next morning, after a light but refreshing breakfast of sharp berries and early fruits, which bore a little resemblance to strawberries but tasted not nearly as sweet, they convened in the main pyramid.

Mithras was talking keenly to Arion, and when he saw Simon and Flora enter sleepily, Johnny and Anna behind them, he nodded curtly and said, 'Good. I must show you something.'

He walked up to the altar and knelt before it. Simon thought he must have pressed a lever or a button, as the front face of the altar swung away, revealing a black pane of glass.

Arion followed Mithras; the others – Cautes hobbling on a wooden crutch Arion had found in the priests' infirmary – gathered in front of the altar steps.

'I was using it before, but then after the king died I couldn't make it work,' said Arion.

'Try it,' said Mithras.

Frowning slightly, Arion sat cross-legged in front of it, and closed his eyes. Then he reached out and touched the glass.

The blackness cleared, and a view opened out in the glass.

'The capital city!' said Flora.

There it was: they watched a small band of knights in black armour, walking through the streets, the people scattering before them. Then Lavinia, the Lady of the Stag, was leading a charge against them.

'It's worse than I thought,' said Selena. She considered the scene for a moment, then glanced at Mithras, who nodded almost imperceptibly. 'I must return. The people need me.'

The picture switched, first to a rocky, forbidding, storm-swept mountain with crumbling rocks tumbling down its sides; then a calm, sunlit sea, on which sailing ships with golden sails passed. Then a surge grew in the waves, boiling upwards and scattering the ships. The image shifted, and they saw four girls, pasty-faced and placid, sitting sewing in a large tower room – at which Selena started, and said, 'My sisters! I hope they are safe . . .'

The scene changed before they could see anything more, and there was a forest, with someone tall and dark-skinned running through it. 'I don't recognise those kinds of trees . . .' said Selena. 'Those are not of the kingdom, surely. Can you stop it, Arion? Make it go back to my sisters? To the city? I must find out what is going on.'

'I can't control it,' said Arion, gritting his teeth.

It flickered and for one brief, glorious moment Simon and Anna saw their own cottage by the sea. They saw their parents, asleep in their bed, suspended in a golden light. But as they watched, the light began to darken, and a horned shadow spread over their sleeping bodies.

'No!' shouted Simon.

Arion broke his connection, and the picture returned to blackness.

'The king's in there somewhere, some remnant of him,' said Simon.

'Mummy and Daddy! Are they OK?' whispered Anna, peering out from behind Cautes.

'I don't know,' said Mithras. 'Does your device always tell the truth?'

Arion sighed. 'It has not yet failed.'

'But does it show the present or the future?' asked Simon.

'I don't know,' replied Arion. 'I would normally be able to check, but it's all wrong. I can't understand it or control it as I used to be able to.'

They all understood. It was the king's trap, spreading through the worlds, his shadow reaching far.

Mithras lifted his hands to his face, and when he took them down, Simon saw that he looked drawn and pale. 'Time is running out,' said Mithras. 'The king has let something loose . . . We must make haste to stop it, or all will be lost.'

Outside in the morning air Selena seemed confident, but Simon could not help noticing how tired she looked. She hooded her head, covering up her horns, and sprang on to her horned horse, with panniers laden on either side.

Selena addressed the little band as she turned her horse to the south and the direction of Notus. 'I leave you with Mithras. Remember: the safety of all the worlds is at stake. I bid you luck and speed. We shall meet and sing before the blossom lines the trees in the palace square.' Without another word, she kicked into the flanks of her horse and galloped off.

They stood in silence for a while, watching her, until she was nothing but a small dot; then they turned to go back into the glass pyramid.

When they were inside, Mithras said, 'Arion. We must reach the Centre of the Worlds – the realm of the goddess. We must find her there. Do you know how to do it?'

Arion shook his head and buried his chin in his shoulder. When he looked up, a few seconds later, he said, 'I'm sorry, my lord, I do not.'

Simon's heart sank and he watched the faces of the others grow strained. Was there no hope at all?

'But,' Arion continued slowly, 'I think I know where we can find out.'

'Then take us there,' said Mithras. 'Now.'

Chapter Eight

THE

BLACK ALTAR

'NOT HERE . . .' Arion was saying. 'Nor here . . .'
He ran his finger over the spines of a shelf
full of leather-bound books.

They were in the temple's library, a huge square
room filled with tall bookcases between glass
windows that looked out on to the mountains. Up
above them was a dome, tooled with golden symbols
of the moon and the north wind.

Anna was delighting in the books, taking out the
ones that were at her level, reading the spines and
flicking through pages. Occasionally she would stop
and put her finger in a book as if to mark it, then she

would find something else and move on.

Arion's finger stopped. 'Here. This shelf is all I know we have about that kind of working – the deep kind, that also made your horn, Simon, and Flora's sunsword, and the shadow-spheres you carry.'

'Cautes and I will look through these.' Mithras hefted up a huge pile of thick books, and coughed as the dust filled his nostrils. 'Arion, you look through those.' The boy priest picked up a huge volume and almost dropped it. He put it down on the floor and opened it. Simon saw it was written in symbols, like those around the circles of the three worlds he'd seen in the Temple Cave back in the city.

Cautes limped to a table, laid out a tome, and began to read. Anna, who had taken a fancy to him, sat by him with a book of her own, and from time to time he stroked her hair absently as she played with her doll and flicked through some of the pages. There were diagrams that pleased her, and drawings she could understand.

'All we know is that there *is* a way to get to the home of the Threefold Goddess,' said Arion. 'But none has used it – save King Selenus. When he tore his shadow from the goddess, he became changed beyond measure.' He bent his head to the book he was holding, and he and Mithras became absorbed in their tasks.

The others, feeling useless, went back into the main temple. They began to tidy where they could, sweeping up, and looking at the statues and decorations around them.

The sun was climbing up towards the middle of the sky when they halted for a break. Simon, wiping the sweat off his brow with the back of his hand, stepped outside and breathed in the cool mountain air. At the edge of his eyesight, he sensed something moving in the bushes.

'Anna,' he called out. 'Stop messing about and come here.'

The bushes rattled, and then were still. In the silence Simon wasn't sure if the sound he then heard was someone giggling or not.

When the first pebble struck him, he was mildly annoyed. When the second pinged him on the skull, causing a fierce pain to sear through his head, he became enraged, and ran towards the bushes.

'Anna! Stop it!' he roared, crashing into the undergrowth.

There was nobody there, but something gripped his legs, and suddenly the ground was above him, and he was swinging from side to side, head down. A clamp was around his calves, and he glimpsed something hideous skittering away into the bushes. He shouted weakly, and heard Flora coming towards him.

The trap was simple but powerful. The rope was biting into him, and when Mithras and Pike reached Simon, he was still flailing. They released him gently, and bore him back into the temple.

He wasn't badly hurt, but the shock had been deep.

'The mantrap! I'm sorry, I set it up a while ago to protect the temple,' said Arion when they came in.

'Something led me to it,' said Simon. 'On purpose.' He winced.

'I cannot use much of my energy to help you,' said Mithras, shaking his head. 'I must save myself to defend this world whilst you are gone.' But he did place his hand on Simon's head, and Simon felt a gentle healing warmth pervade his body.

'Did you see what it was?' asked Cautes.

'No,' said Simon. 'But I have a horrible feeling it was one of those monkey things . . . the king's pets. I think I saw them before in the forest.'

'But why?' said Pike. 'Do they want revenge on us?'

'Perhaps,' said Mithras. 'We must be careful. There may be a disgruntled knight tracking us – one of the king's supporters, perhaps one of Ursus's men.'

They made sure the perimeter of the temple was secure, and set up a rota of guards.

At dinner, they found that the researchers had got no further with their task, although Anna was looking pleased with herself. When asked why she was so happy, she would only shake her head and look mysteriously at her doll.

As they were desultorily picking at their salads and sweet root vegetables, the shadows on the table shimmered. Simon shivered instinctively, but a magehawk flew through from the black, clasping in its beak a message. Mithras took it, unwrapped it, and scanned the writing quickly.

'From Selena. She has caught up with Lucia and her band. So that is a relief at least. She will have protection now, and they will reach the city within three or four days – less, if they ride fast.'

He scribbled a reply, and put it carefully in the magehawk's beak; it shook its wings, and then it was gone.

'We will work through the night,' said Mithras.

'Can you teach us how to read that stuff?' asked Flora.

Mithras hesitated. 'Not in the time we have, but you can look through the books we have already searched. Who knows – it may be of use. You never know with these books of workings. You might recognise some pattern or shape that we have missed.'

'I can see how to do some things,' said Anna. 'Some of it's easy. You can tell from the pictures.' Mithras patted her head and, furious, she went away sulking to the other side of the room.

So they all sat in the library, candles lit all about them; Flora with her back to one of the gigantic shelves; Simon, legs smarting, on a window seat, and everyone busily read.

At first Simon thought there was no point in doing it. How could he find the secret here? He didn't know the language, couldn't read the symbols. It all looked like nonsense to him.

He started to feel drowsy whilst the quiet scratch and flicker of pages being turned went on around him. He finished looking through the books that Mithras had already seen, and then got up to look at the other shelves, idly picking out a couple more.

He stared at the symbols, and they made no sense in his mind. *Foolishness*, he thought. *I can't do this*. He let his eyes wander over the diagrams.

He relaxed into a state of contemplation, and drifted into a reverie, turning over the pages but not really taking in what was on them. There was a figure like a man, blowing out his cheeks; writing that was all squiggles and loops; a black square; those three interlocking circles.

He drifted further. Soon, he realised something strange was happening. The quiet spaces of the library were fading away. He saw, as in a vision, a great, long, black altar, and beneath it was a fire.

Something horrible was on the fire, but he couldn't make out what it was. There were three figures rising up and joining hands, and they danced around the altar.

Dimly he perceived that he ought to know who the three people were, and it was with a gentle lurch that he realised it was Flora, Pike and himself.

They danced around faster and faster until they were passing almost in a blur. Simon couldn't make out any individual features; it was as if he, Flora and Pike were becoming one person, united in a flowing loop of movement.

Smoke billowed from under the stone altar, twisting around the three dancers, enveloping them, smothering them.

The dancers vanished from sight.

The library returned around Simon. He sat up, his attention piqued, and he looked back at the book.

'Mithras,' he said, readjusting himself to the scene actually around him. The vision had come as he'd gazed at the book – perhaps there was something in it. 'Come here . . .' He showed Mithras the book he was holding. Mithras took it, pushed it back at him – then snatched it again quickly.

'Wait,' he said. 'Yes . . . I've been reading this wrongly. This is a different dialect . . . the older language of the priests. How stupid of me not to notice!' He looked up. 'Well, Simon, you have done it. You have found the way to get to the Centre of the Worlds – to the abode of the goddess herself!'

Chapter Nine

BLOOD
SACRIFICE

MITHRAS CONTINUED TO scan the page of the book Simon had found, his expression darkening. He looked up gravely and met Simon's eyes. 'I would be joyful at finding what we sought. But now I see what is to come, and it gives me great fear.'

The others gathered around as Mithras carefully examined its pages. He held the book as if it were an animal, with great tenderness and care.

'Here we are,' he said, finding what he was looking for. '*In time of great need it is possible to visit the goddess herself.*' Mithras paused whilst he read on. 'We need blood from one person of each of the realms. And then we make a black altar, and under it light a fire built from bitterwood grown in the orchards of the priests of Boreas. We sprinkle it with dust from the Jagged Tower of Eurus; with sea salt from the Port of Notus; and honeywort from the Bay of Zephyrus. We need also a shadow . . . That might cause us trouble.'

'The shadow-spheres!' said Simon eagerly.

'Excellent,' said Mithras. 'There are other ingredients, but nothing we will not find here, I think. The door is then opened – briefly. Those wishing to enter drink from a vial of the blood, mixed with wine.'

Arion went over to a sideboard and opened it, coming back with a bottle. 'Fortified wine,' he said. 'Will it do?'

Mithras nodded. 'And you then enter, but the path is only opened for a short while, and you must make all speed to the goddess, discover what is happening, and free her. The objects you take with you will also travel alongside you.'

'Have you done this ritual before?' asked Simon.

Mithras shook his head. 'I certainly haven't. Is there any record of a Borean priest doing it?'

Arion looked pale. 'I think one tried but . . .' He didn't have to finish the sentence. Everyone understood. The only person who had done it successfully had been the old king.

This was his revenge. He knew that his death would bring down the worlds around him, and death or worse would await anyone who tried to stop it from happening.

'Are you sure you want to do this?' said Mithras.

'Yes,' answered Simon. Pike clasped Simon's hand, and Flora joined them. Johnny bristled a little, stretching his lanky body. 'I have to come too,' he said. 'You'll need help.'

'And I will offer my assistance,' said Cautes, 'maimed though I am, I will be able to use some of my energy, I hope.'

'My poor children,' said Mithras. 'That it should ever come to this . . . You must give me your blood first.'

Simon held out his hand, palm upwards, and Mithras pricked his thumb, collecting two drops in a vial. Cautes offered his, but Mithras shook his head and did it to himself; then he took the same amount of blood from Pike, who didn't even flinch. Stopping up the vial, Mithras placed it beside the altar.

It was getting light; the sun was rising and spilling its silver rays into the library. Arion went out into the temple orchard with an axe to chop off some branches of bitterwood for the fire, whilst Mithras departed to the storerooms to look for the rest of the ingredients.

The others remained in the library. Anna sat under a table, playing resolutely with her doll and muttering quietly to herself. She had one of the books open by her feet, and she was putting the doll through various positions.

Cautes threw his arms around Simon and Flora, and they felt some warmth from him, but Simon could not suppress the anxiety that was bubbling in his heart. He felt as if he were standing on the edge of an abyss, bigger and deeper and stranger than anything he'd ever seen before.

What might lurk in the home of the goddess? What might roam the spaces between worlds? If that creature they'd fought in the pass was anything to go by then their quest would be finished.

As if sensing his disturbance, Cautes said, 'I will be with you.'

Simon, thanking Cautes, went to Anna and clutched her tightly to him.

'Don't want you to go,' she whispered.

'I have to, Anna,' said Simon. 'I have to. And I promise, I promise on my life, that I will be back and we will go home together and eat baked beans and jump up and down on Mummy and Daddy's bed.'

'Johnny gets to go . . .' said Anna.

'I know, I know . . . but I promise I'll be back, OK?'

He held her hand gently, and then embraced her fully.

Arion returned a few minutes later looking breathless, carrying some slender branches. 'I think someone's outside . . .' he said. 'I heard something, maybe like laughter, something scuttling in the bushes.'

'Then all the more reason to hurry,' replied Mithras, sweeping in, his arms full of caskets and boxes. He placed them carefully on a table. 'We're lucky. Your stores had everything we needed. These were untouched.'

'Never had use for them before,' said Arion. He piled up the branches in the centre of the library.

Mithras drew an oblong on the ground around the branches, and calmly placed four books of the same size at each corner. He turned to Simon and asked him to help, and the two of them went into the main pyramid, up to the altar.

They removed one of its sides easily enough, and carried it back in and positioned it on top of the books. It was a black, glinting thing, and Simon did not like to see his reflection in it.

'We have our altar,' said Mithras. 'Now all we need is Johnny.'

The sound of shattering glass came to their ears. A moment passed, and then Johnny came hurtling into the room.

'We're under attack! Those monkey creatures – they're throwing rocks into the pyramid! And there's someone else – a knight, I'm sure of it. I couldn't quite see him, but he was definitely wearing armour.'

Mithras told them to wait where they were, and ran out into the main hall. There was the sound of muffled shrieks, more crashing, and a few seconds later Mithras rushed back in, closing the door behind him.

'There's a knight there – young, but vicious-looking, with two companions. And something else – something from another realm. The knight has somehow brought it to the temple.'

'What do we do? Shall we fight them off? We have weapons!' exclaimed Pike.

Mithras looked worried. 'There's nothing for it,' he said. 'We have to do the ceremony – now – before they get any further into the temple. We'll get you through and I'll fend off this attack.'

Pike ran to the door and began piling furniture against it, Johnny and Cautes helping him.

Anna started to wail.

'What do we need to do?' asked Simon. 'Arion, quickly!'

Arion thumbed through the book as fast as he could. 'Light the fire . . .'

Mithras stepped forwards, gathered himself, reaching deep into his stores of energy, and touched his hand to the branches. They flickered and suddenly burst into bright, golden flames. He looked greyer afterwards, but did not waver in his intent.

'Sprinkle the dust.' More glass broke in the main pyramid. 'The temple!' shouted Arion, distracted.

'Don't worry, we'll repair it afterwards,' Mithras called. The flames flared with a greenish tinge as he threw the dust over the fire, then filled the room with a beautiful scent of honey when the honeywort went in, before glowing blue in reply to the sea salt.

'Do you have everything you need?' called Arion.

Flora, Pike and Simon checked themselves. They had the sunsword and the hunting horn; they had the shadow-spheres. Each had a sword and a dagger at their belts, and a small shield strapped to their back, bows and arrows.

'Get ready!' called Arion.

Cautes gently took hold of Simon's hand, and signalled to him to grab Flora. He did, and Johnny came between Flora and Cautes. Mithras gave the vial of blood and wine to them, and they each took a sip, trying not to think about it too much.

Arion called out to them. 'Circle the altar clockwise once!'

They did so, the sound of the destruction of the temple reaching their ears, sounding louder, closer.

'Now widdershins!'

They turned, and Simon almost felt like laughing as Arion began calling out the turns, their movements absurdly joyful and dancelike, even with the hobbling Cautes. 'Three times forwards! Once back! Three times forwards! Once back!'

Mithras, reaching over the dancing group, placed one of the little shadow-spheres on the top of the black altar, and as they circled it, it began to grow.

It became the size of an egg, then a boulder. In it appeared strange lights and swirling patterns, pulsing gently with ripples and movements.

'Three times forwards . . .'

Something fell in the great pyramid, and there was a roaring sound, as of someone shouting in triumph. The furniture stacked against the door shivered.

'The final part . . .' said Arion, his voice trembling. 'Mithras? Are you ready?'

Mithras nodded, his expression unreadable. He'd carefully laid out a knife on the surface of the table next to him, and now picked it up.

The sphere pulsed, the dancers went round and round, their minds dizzied, part of a force greater than the sum of themselves.

With a sudden movement, Mithras made a deep wound in his flank, catching the blood in a goblet, and pouring it on to the black sphere which absorbed it with a sucking noise.

'The blood of a holy one of the Golden Realm,' whispered Arion, 'to be given unto its last drop!'

'No! Mithras!' Cautes called.

'When the king did this before,' said Mithras, 'he used a noble of the Realm, taken against her will and murdered. And we felt her loss deeply. And now it must be me,' he continued calmly. 'You cannot stop the ritual!'

The sphere grew ever more wide. Its membrane stretched, and soon it was half a finger's breadth away from the faces of the dancers. Mithras grew faint as the blood poured out of him, as the intruders battered against the door.

Arion struggled to place more things in front of the library door, stacking up books, anything he could lay his hands on.

'Arion . . .' spluttered Mithras. 'After this, take Anna, leave this place. Go to the village and there wait.'

The door shook in its frame, and burst open, pushing back the stacked-up chairs so that they toppled and fell to the floor.

Arion jumped backwards. In came Cygnet with the monkey creatures. There was something else behind him, black and huge and bear-like. It reached out as if fumbling, moving slowly around the room.

Mithras summoned all his strength. The sphere enveloped the dancers, now indistinguishable in the darkness, a black heart to the great confusion spilling in the library.

Arion was running at Cygnet, wielding a chair leg above his head. Cygnet simply stepped out of the way, ignoring him and staring with fascination at the black sphere. Blood oozing from his wound, Mithras staggered and fell.

The figures in the shadow became fainter, and the sphere began to shrink.

'Where do they go, O holy one?' asked Cygnet. Behind him the black thing slid towards Mithras, and the monkey creatures ran about, throwing things and pulling books off shelves.

'Do not follow them,' gasped Mithras. 'Stay your vengeance. More is at stake than you know.' He crawled towards the vial, and reached out a hand to grab it.

'So that's it, is it? You have to drink from that?'

Cygnet snatched it up before Mithras could reach it. Mithras let out a groan.

As the dancers faded, Cygnet made a decision. He picked up the vial of mingled blood and wine, and sipped from it; then, dropping it, pushed through the membrane of the sphere without a backwards glance.

Mithras fell to the ground as a wave of energy burst from the shadow-sphere. Arion ran to his side and attempted to staunch his wound whilst the monkey creatures gibbered in terror, or joy, he could not tell.

Shrinking, the sphere hung briefly in the air, before falling and coming to a perfect stop on the black altar.

The dancers had gone.

The black beast that Cygnet had captured and released into the library hissed, and rumbled towards Mithras.

Summoning his last reserves of strength, Mithras sent a wave of golden energy at the beast, hitting it right in the centre.

It screamed, a long, terrible sound, then hissed, flailing its limbs everywhere before it curled into itself, and vanished.

The chattering monkey creatures fled through the open door, hooting as they went.

Fainting, Mithras collapsed.

'What do we do now?' sobbed Arion.

'My blood . . .'

'Mithras! Please! You cannot die!'

'Anna – find Anna . . .'

Leaving Mithras reluctantly, Arion searched around the library, calling for her.

There was no sign of her. Where she'd been sitting were some books, one with a page torn out. He studied it, but found no clue as to what it might mean. On the other leaf was simply a picture of a puppet, loose and dangling, lying on the ground. He shut the book.

As Arion came back to help staunch Mithras's wound, he stumbled on something. It was the vial, right by the table where she'd been hiding. He picked it up. It was empty. His heart fluttered.

Arion went to Mithras, whose eyes were now shut, all colour drained from his face. That once proud, handsome, golden head was empty and wan. Arion held Mithras's hand as the last drops of blood stained the tourniquet he'd made, and Mithras's breathing grew ever slower.

'Mithras . . .' Arion whispered, and bent low to cradle the dying demi-god in his arms.

PART TWO

THE CENTRE
OF THE WORLDS

Chapter Ten

INTERZONE

LIGHTS. STRONG, UNWAVERING. Were they torches? Or lamps? Or even windows? Something strange in the atmosphere, as if the walls were breathing. A long, dark corridor, bending and stretching away into the distance in both directions.

Cautes went first, still hobbling on his crutch and helped by Johnny, and Simon, Flora and Pike in a trio behind them.

The five of them stumbled up a slope, and realised they could not be inside anything, because they were being buffeted by winds – cold, strong winds whose iciness drilled deep into their bones.

They were conscious of their bodies; they were breathing, the spit was wet in their mouths and blood was thrumming in their temples.

Sounds, murmurs, on the edge of hearing. Voices. But were they voices? Again, a feeling that everything was trembling.

A dim light glowed ahead – the golden glow spread into the shape of Cautes, and Simon was glad for his light. 'Follow us!' called Cautes.

They struggled onwards, no one knowing if they would ever come out of this strange place. The glimmering lights on either side of them sometimes glowed red, or blue, or green. Johnny felt he might be deep in some hallucination. Pike looked around, full of wonder.

Simon patted the hunting horn strapped to his body while Flora fingered the hilt of the sunsword at her belt, both wondering if their weapons would work in this place.

Cautes flared up his outline again. He was standing, waiting with Johnny, and Simon was the first to reach him, and he could not help throwing himself into Cautes's arms.

The others, dim shapes in the gloom, approached slowly. Flora appeared next, looking grey and determined, and then finally Pike, whose eyes were shining with an apprehension that Simon had never seen in him before.

'Where are we?' said Simon.

'I have heard tell of this place,' answered Cautes. 'Some call it the Interzone. In the Golden Realm, we were experimenting with it to reach the Silver Kingdom. It is dangerous, and we must not stay here. There are strange powers. You see these lights? They are markers of worlds. One will lead us to the home of the goddess. Another will lead us back to the Temple of the Priests of Boreas.'

'How can we tell which is which?' *There might be a way back home from here,* thought Simon. *But using it would be impossible – the whole universe will die . . .*

Cautes looked thoughtful. 'The only way is to try them . . .'

'But there are hundreds! Where do the others lead?' wondered Flora.

'Who knows?' said Cautes. 'Places I have never dreamed of . . .'

The wind was getting colder; it bit into their skin. They felt dislocated. Simon wasn't sure of his body or his mind. He grabbed on to Flora for comfort.

'The shadow-spheres came from the home of

the goddess, didn't they?' said Flora, remembering what she'd once been told. 'Maybe they can help?'

Simon had carried them in his pocket, and he pulled one out. They continued steadily upwards, following Cautes, whose dimly glowing outline was beginning to flicker. 'I can't keep up the energy much longer,' he said, leaning on his crutch.

Soon enough, his radiance faded, and their dark path was lit only by the ever-changing lights. Flora pulled out the sunsword but it didn't glow, and she resheathed it, uneasily.

Simon held the shadow-sphere out in front of him. Little lights of red, then green, then blue danced within its depths, sometimes merging, sometimes jumping apart. But he wasn't sure what to make of it.

Someone bumped into him, and for a moment he didn't recognise the face of the girl in front of him. Simon shook his head and blinked. Flora. It was Flora, his friend, staring at him vaguely.

She put out a hand. 'I'm Flora Williamson. I'm looking for . . .' She paused, puzzled. Then Johnny bumped into her and grabbed her.

'It's all right, sis, I'm here,' he said.

'Urgh,' Flora said suddenly. 'That was horrible!

It was like having a bit of my brain removed.'

'Being in this place is starting to have an effect on us!' shouted Cautes. 'We should not linger. Simon, any luck?'

Simon noticed that the dancing lights in the shadow-sphere were glowing brighter as they walked. There were shapes, indistinct – was that a horse? Or a winged horse? An eagle, perhaps? 'I think so,' said Simon. 'I think . . .'

And then he forgot who he was, and where he was, and he was simply staring at a black sphere in his hand whilst all around him strangers stood with their mouths open, babbling weird words.

'Cmonsmon,' said a blond man. 'Thnk!'

The circle of people looked at him. Their lips were moving; some of them were reaching out to him. He was frightened, and stepped back from them, holding up his hands as if to ward them off.

'Smnismeeflora,' said another of the things, long black hair flopping around its face.

The creature took his shoulder and shook him. Something about the eyes, looking at him imploringly, jogged him. This wasn't a creature, spewing out meaningless noises. It had a name. It was a girl. Talking to him.

And slowly, like swimming through thick oil, his memory came back to him. The moment passed, and he knew himself and the others once more.

'Focus!' said Cautes.

'I . . . think that the lights in the shadow-sphere are getting stronger. Maybe it glows fully when we're near the right entrance. Look!'

And it began to emanate a blue glow, as they neared a blue light up ahead. Within the blue glow were now three distinct shapes: an eagle, a horse and a woman.

'This must be it,' said Cautes, looking at the shadow-sphere. 'We've got to take the risk. The threefold goddess's forms are in the sphere. I . . . er . . . I . . .' And even he looked for a moment as if he had completely forgotten who or what he was. Then resolve strengthened his face. 'Let's go in. Pike, you first. I'll go last.'

Gritting his teeth, Pike stepped into the blue light to the side of them, and vanished from sight. The rest followed, and Cautes, wiping the sweat off his brow, staggered through after them.

Cygnet, who had been just behind them in the dark, was about to follow when he heard, very faintly, the sobbing of a child. He paused, trying to ignore it, but the sound came again, and, moreover, was obviously from a small girl. His mind felt strange and light. For a moment he forgot who he was, and then the image of his father, proud and tall, bending to give him a hawk from his wrist, pulled him back to himself.

A huddled, shadowy shape drew his attention. He went towards it, and the shape resolved itself into that boy's little sister, Anna. Despite himself, a slow smile spread across Cygnet's lips.

'Little girl,' he said in his softest tones. 'What ails you?'

Anna looked up. 'Who are you?' she said uncertainly. 'I don't know where I am . . . I'm not sure . . .' She trailed off.

Cygnet's mind started to wander again, but once more his father's face came before his eyes and he remembered his task.

'I am one who will help you,' he replied. 'Will you come with me?'

Anna clutched her doll to her chest, and for a moment Cygnet thought that the doll had nestled even closer to her of its own accord, but it must simply have been a trick of the light in this strange place.

'A fair lady,' he said. 'What is her name?'

'I . . . I don't remember. We're lost. We're looking for . . . We came here with my . . . I just want to go home! I'm so cold, and I don't know where I am.'

She began crying again, huge, gulping howls, and Cygnet knelt to comfort her.

'There, there,' he said awkwardly. 'Come with me, and I will bring you to where you need to go, and all will be well.'

A pretty little hostage, he thought, and he led Anna to the blue light. Together they stepped into its reach.

Chapter Eleven

THE
SHIFTING WORLD

AFTER THEY'D GONE through the blue light, the five travellers found themselves in a valley. A cold, black stream ran through it, shimmering rocks rose on either side of them. The next moment, without having moved at all, they were in a forest, and all the trees had blue leaves, and strange creatures shivered away from them in the undergrowth.

'What's going on?' shouted Simon, grabbing on to a tree.

'I don't know,' replied Cautes. 'Everybody hold hands. Don't let go.'

Cautes leaned on his crutch and held Simon's

hand, Simon clung to Flora, who in turn held Johnny, and Johnny gripped on to Pike's right hand.

The blue forest became a large plain covered in long, waving grasses, and huge red flowers that turned towards an orange sun.

Walking in a chain, each turned to check that the other was still behind. Simon felt as if he himself might shift and change with the scenery, might become someone or something else.

They walked on and felt the grasses rub against their skin. The flowers were humming, seeming to sing, and butterflies were joining in. When the notes harmonised, the butterflies would find a flower and sit, sipping daintily from the cup of its petals.

In the grassland moved beasts that seemed completely oblivious of them. They were green, and had huge plated heads like pangolins. One of them extended a long, sticky tongue, and pulled up a tussock of grass by the root.

Just as suddenly, the grassland morphed into desert, and the heat of a huge sun beat down on them.

'I'm thirsty,' said Johnny.

As they fought their way through the sand dunes, everything rippled again, and now they were in a village, its houses lying in ruins, and nothing moving in the streets around them. It was cool, and the sky was grey. A light rain fell upon them, and they let it wet their lips. A low, yellow sun was partly obscured by clouds.

Looking around, it took a moment for Simon to realise. 'This looks like Limerton!' he said. 'Where we lived on Earth. Are we there? Have we gone back? Is it . . . gone?'

Cautes shook his head. 'We're in the realm of the goddess, where every world is possible, in every form. Time and space do not mean the same things here as they do where you come from.'

They paused at the village green, and Simon felt a pang of terrible longing as he recognised the pub and the church, dilapidated and broken as they were.

'We should press on,' said Simon. He didn't need to add that he felt decidedly uncomfortable.

Cautes nodded. 'You're right. But first we need to work out a plan. How on earth are we going to find the goddess?'

Simon located the shadow-sphere in his pocket to see if it could help them. It was cold and inert. The sunsword, when unsheathed, gave off the dimmest of light. They sat down to think about how to go on, and then almost immediately the world shivered, shifting the landscape once more.

They were now on a beach, the blue-black sea washing against the shore; the sky was dead slate grey. The sand was heaving with a mass of black crabs, all waving their pincers and scuttling angrily towards them.

The friends were instantly on their feet, and Cautes yelled at them to stand still. It was very hard to do so; the creatures were so menacing. As they scurried nearer, Simon was horrified to see that they had little furry heads like bats, and were showing pointed teeth.

The crabs advanced, and Simon was sure that as the horde passed them the little faces hissed and spat at him. They made a curious sound as they went, clicking like bones in a bag, almost as if they were communicating with each other. They surged around the travellers, passing in between them, so close that they brushed their clothes.

The horde grew distant and soon only some little ones were left clattering along; they hopped past quickly, rushing after their comrades. Then the last one went over the brow of a cliff, and everybody relaxed.

'Wait,' said Flora. 'What's that?' She pointed

along the beach to where the crabs had come from. Something large and black was moving slowly towards them. It was huge, as big as a horse, it had six strong, armoured legs, and was bristling with fur. It had the same bat-face, and its fangs were long and sharp.

'I think that must be Mother . . .' said Cautes.

The creature came closer to the shivering group. They could not turn and run – the horde was behind them; the mother crab barred their way in front; the surf sounded to the left. 'We must stay and face the beast,' said Cautes.

Soon it was within a few paces of where they stood. A cool wind blew over them. The beast stank of salt and flesh, and something deeper and ranker.

Simon looked at the others and imagined that they were thinking the same as he was: *What a death, crushed by those monstrous fangs.* 'Cautes . . .' he said quietly. 'Don't you think we should –?' He was about to say 'run', when the beast opened its maw.

'*Rrrrawwwwk!*' The beast made a noise, its mouth foaming and dripping with saliva.

Cautes went towards it, and to the horror of those watching, reached out a hand, touching the beast on its head.

But then a strange thing happened. The beast knelt. It put its ears forwards, and seemed to be concentrating deeply.

After a while, in which the others shifted uncomfortably, Cautes turned to the group. 'Her name, as far as I can make it out, is She-who-rakes-the-shores. She says she is from the goddess,' he said. 'She received a message to find us, and has been searching for us since we entered the realm. She says now that we have met, the world will stop shifting. She knows where the mare is kept, and she can lead us to her.'

'How did you manage that?' said Flora.

'I think you call it telepathy,' said Cautes. 'It was a bit of a fad when we were last, properly, in your world . . .'

She-who-rakes-the-shores croaked again and lumbered around, and the little group began to follow her. Johnny was lagging behind, pondering, staring at the sandy beach beneath his feet as he went. Cautes took the lead, limping along lopsidedly beside the creature. Simon walked three abreast with Flora on his left, and Pike striding on his right.

They passed over the brow of a sand dune, and pressed on in the wake of the beast. *Cautes trusts her,* thought Simon, *so she must be all right.* But as they walked he could not help but feel apprehensive.

A little while later, Cygnet and Anna appeared.

Cygnet peered at the footsteps on the sand. He was confused. He had lost sight of his quarry, and he did not know what was happening. Everything kept changing, confusing him. Anna had gone quiet, and for some reason he found this much more worrying than if she had been wailing and crying.

'I think these are their footsteps,' said Cygnet, partly to himself, and partly to Anna. 'They went over this way.'

'What if everything changes again?' said Anna. 'How do you even know it's them and not something else?' Anna's doll was clutched tightly in her hand.

'We will find them,' said Cygnet.

And when we do, he thought, *I wonder what they will give to have her back . . .*

Chapter Twelve

INSECTS
AND ACID

THE SAND WAS dry; their footprints left deep impressions. The sun, a fat orange ball wreathed in mist, shone hotly. The little group walked slowly.

They hadn't gone far when Pike suddenly made a strangulated yelping noise, as if he'd been stung by a wasp.

'What was that?' he said, casting around.

'I can't see anything,' said Simon.

Then Flora felt a sharp sting on the back of her hand, and she squealed too. 'Do they have mosquitoes here?' she asked. But there was no sign of anything that might have caused it.

She-who-rakes-the-shores shivered, and lifted her bat-head to the sky. '*Rrraaaawwwk!*'

'What does that mean?' said Simon.

Cautes looked at them. 'It means – broadly speaking – run as fast as you can to the cave under the lip of that sand dune!'

A shadow crept over the sun, and everybody looked upwards. A mass of insects was above them. Only these were not the size of an average fly or wasp, or even the large hornet that Simon had once seen in Suffolk.

These were as big as a newborn hound, and they were buzzing angrily. They had large stingers protruding from their backs, and small drops of venom were falling from them.

Simon gasped as a drop hit him, burned through his clothes and on to his skin. 'It's acid! They're spewing acid! Everyone, run!'

They sprinted to the shelter of the rock, and She-who-rakes-the-shores took up guard at the cave entrance.

The insects swarmed, and hovered in the air above them.

'The sunsword! Try it!' suggested Cautes.

Flora unsheathed it and stepped out, taking

careful aim as one of the insects flew at her. The sword clanged into its side, and the insect was thrown off course, but nothing more than that. Its exoskeleton was clearly hard, and the sword was not at full strength.

Flora ducked back down behind She-who-rakes-the-shores once more. 'Cautes, what can we do?'

Cautes gulped and pointed. Beneath the hovering crowd, the sand was melting away as the acid poured on to it.

One of the larger insects swooped down upon She-who-rakes-the-shores, and spat acid at her head.

She-who-rakes-the-shores roared, and stood up on her hind legs, blotting out their view of the beach. And then she charged at the insects, snapping about with the pincers on her top pair of limbs. They watched in horror as she caught one and sliced it in half. It fell to the ground, shuddering and spilling out acid from its stinger all over the sand, dissolving it until there was a large hole and nothing but smoking remains.

Howling, the insects dived at She-who-rakes-the-shores.

'We have to help her,' said Flora shakily.

'Cover up your faces,' said Cautes. They wrapped

T-shirts and cloth around their heads until they resembled Arab raiders. 'Pull out your weapons. Try to keep your skin covered. Charge at them and aim for their bellies or their heads, where they have no protection. If you get acid on you, retreat immediately.' He pulled deep into his reserves of energy, and a weak golden glow emanated from him. 'Ready?'

They attacked. Johnny went flailing at the first insect he saw, and managed to damage its wings with his sword. Flora, practised now with the sunsword, disabled two in a row by hitting them in the soft part of their heads. Simon and Pike were knocking into as many as they could, batting them away. Cautes strode forwards, a little wobbly, his energy pushing some of them away with its force, but it was not strong enough to repel many.

Roaring, She-who-rakes-the-shores snapped another insect in half, but more came at her. Three alighted on her back and began to spray acid over her; she screamed in pain.

'Cautes!' called Pike, just in time as a large insect swooped behind him and let spray. Cautes managed to block it with a small shield that hissed and started to crumble.

The swarm of insects regrouped itself and formed above the shoreline. They were waiting for the final moment, readying themselves to attack and eliminate. The buzzing of their wings was metallic and dissonant.

She-who-rakes-the-shores was groaning in pain. Cautes tried to pass on some of his energy to her, but he was weak, and he could barely retain enough to keep himself standing.

'The only thing we can do is run,' gasped Johnny.

'But where? They'll be on us in a second,' said Flora.

And it was then that they began to feel truly frightened.

One by one, the huge insects extended their stingers and began to soar in a curve towards the cave where the friends stood, facing outwards, holding their ineffective weapons in front of them.

In desperation, Simon sounded the hunting horn, but what came out was little more than a rasp, and he fell back, pale and trembling.

The closest of the insects dived towards them, its shadow large and looming on the sand. She-who-rakes-the-shores's skin was steaming with acid, blood oozing from the wounds.

The buzzing was now louder than a waterfall's roar, and for a second the insect's body filled the space in front of their vision and everything seemed to stop.

They could see the fine bristles on its body, multi-faceted eyes glimmering with different coloured lights, acid dripping from its stinger, its mandibles fierce and cruel.

There was no intelligence in those eyes, nothing but a cold emptiness that did not care whether they lived or died, and was preparing to erase them from the record, as if they had never existed.

Their arms went slack. The insect filled their minds. There was only it, its stinger, and their approaching destruction.

One by one, they fell to their knees; Johnny first, exhausted and bewildered; Flora, holding his hand to comfort him; Pike, fearful; Simon, a ball of confused disappointment in his chest; and then finally Cautes, his glow dimming, his head bowed.

The last thing they heard was the sound of She-who-rakes-the-shores roaring, as if from far off.

Then, abruptly, the insect turned, and flew away. Astonished, they peeped out.

Something was coming over the shoreline.

Something black and huge and moving at a great pace. The insects were dive-bombing it, but whatever it was, it was attacking back.

Flora realised first. 'It's the children! It's She-who-rakes-the-shores's children!'

The whole horde of creatures was rushing to save their mother – called by her voice. In their hundreds and thousands they surged towards the swarm of insects.

Leaping up on to their back legs, the baby crabs nipped and swiped at the insects. One of the insects was caught by the wing, pulled down, and soon there was nothing left of it as the horde poured over its carcass.

'Attack from the back!' shouted Cautes.

Pulling their last reserves of strength together, the little group charged at the diminishing swarm of insects.

Embattled, the insects buzzed here and there, as the crabs jumped up and caught them by the legs or the wings, and the group charged and joined the fray, hitting left and right with abandon. She-who-rakes-the-shores, spurred on by the sight of her children, came rushing in, claws ripping this way and that.

Soon, all but one of the insects had been knocked out of the air. The last hissed once, alarmingly, then fled inland.

The children of She-who-rakes-the-shores flowed around their mother, climbing up her back and over her body. The group watched, astonished, as they covered her with their saliva, tending to her, and her wounds closed.

When they had finished, She-who-rakes-the-shores let out a great roar of delight. '*RRRRAWK!*' she said. '*Rrrawkrrrk?*'

'That means, do we want her children to heal us too?' interpreted Cautes. 'She says their saliva can close our wounds. I wonder if it works with us . . .'

Before he could say anything more, the crabs had already swarmed towards them, and soon they were all covered in little scaly, furry creatures. It wasn't an unpleasant sensation – a bit like having a nice scratch. It was over quickly, and her babies scurried off, back into the dunes. Everyone stretched their limbs out and checked – their wounds had closed.

Cautes and the rest of them thanked She-who-rakes-the-shores. She turned and moved onwards, her legs clicking together as they walked.

Exhausted, they were now turning inland,

scrambling up some scrubby sand dunes that broadened and flattened out into dry grassland. Twilight was approaching. She-who-rakes-the-shores paused at the edge of the dunes and emitted her noise. '*Rrrrawk!*'

Cautes said, 'She can go no further, but the mare lies trapped in the forests up ahead. We are to be careful, as there are things in the forest that she doesn't understand.'

Flora wondered what things such a creature might find difficult to understand, and paled at the thought.

One by one, they bent their heads towards She-who-rakes-the-shores; Cautes put out a hand and stroked the top of her head, and the rest followed suit, finding agreeably soft fur. She seemed pleased, and smiled, or at least, pulled back her lips rather alarmingly. Having seen what those teeth could do, Simon shivered, but he did not shrink back.

They set out across the grassland, and when Simon turned around, he saw She-who-rakes-the-shores, silhouetted by the sun, keeping watch over them as they went.

Chapter Thirteen

THE

BURNING PIT

A T THE EDGE of the forest they found a small, shady clearing, and all threw themselves down on to the ground, apart from Cautes, who lowered himself gently, and looked about for anything that they might be able to eat or drink. There were some dark blue berries hanging from a nearby bush, which he surmised were not poisonous.

Simon went to pick one, and Cautes tasted it carefully. When no ill effects were observed, they shared them out, but it was hardly enough to keep them satisfied. Only Johnny did not want to taste anything, and instead sat by himself with his head in his hands. When Flora went to talk to him, he pushed her away, and, shrugging, she went to join Pike, who was keeping a look out.

Pike almost looks like a man now, thought Simon, *and Flora is harder, stronger. And what has happened to me? Would I recognise myself, if I saw myself in a mirror?* He tried to close his eyes, but his head was full of jagged thoughts, and he could not rest. The dangers ahead of them were vast and unknown. Looking at Johnny, he sensed that Flora's older brother was flailing. But there was nothing he could do about it, and so he put his hand over his eyes, and tried to still his mind.

Meanwhile, Cygnet was slowly making his way across the sands, following their tracks, dragging Anna behind him.

'Look!' said Cygnet. 'Here – they started running. And here – they must have gone into this small cave. A tactical error, surely, for there is no obvious escape. I do not know how long the attack lasted, but there was something big here . . .' Despite himself, he shuddered.

'I would have fought whatever it was,' said Anna, though she was yawning. Her face was white and she had enormous black smudges under her eyes.

'I do not doubt it,' replied Cygnet, sucking air between his teeth.

'When will we catch up with them?' asked Anna as they began to turn inland, following the footprints that were now more evenly spaced out.

'Soon,' replied Cygnet, licking his lips. He had no intention of joining up with them, for the moment at least. He needed to find out more about the place they were in. There was no use challenging them now, when he did not know the lands around them. He would wait, until they were somewhere where he might have more of an advantage. When, as they approached the forest, he saw movement up ahead through the trees, he guessed it was his quarry. He lifted up Anna gently and she let him do so, flopping into his arms like the doll she carried. He turned her head away from the movement, and was surprised to find himself whispering to her, 'It will turn out well.'

She was sluggish, in any case, and Cygnet wondered if, being so small, she was more affected by the travels through worlds than he was. He strode onwards, finding a place not far off from where he could sit and keep watch, and laid Anna down in the roots of a tree, where she remained motionless on her back. Cygnet looked at her for a second, and then turned, gazing through the woods towards the group of travellers, staring into the night.

As soon as dawn broke, the little party, none of whom had slept for any length of time, gathered themselves together and set off through the forest.

Johnny had a blank look on his face; he walked, stumbling, beside Flora, who paced with grim determination, ever ready. Cautes seemed serene, but his face was composed to give the others comfort, and his mind was far away in the Golden Realm, searching his memories for any sliver of help. Pike and Simon went side by side, Pike silent and watchful. Needing Flora's levity, Simon tried to form a joke, but his words felt awkward and uncomfortable, and they died before he could say them.

She-who-rakes-the-shores had told Cautes that the mare was in this forest, and they followed a distinct path that went fairly straight through the centre. The trees surrounding them were thick in their trunks, ancient, with many branches and roots, and large, dark green leaves that swayed and rustled. The orange sun filtered through the leaves, and little black flying things shot in and out of their foliage.

Once they heard a chattering noise, and looked up to see a tiny, rodent-like creature on a branch above them. It had a big bushy tail spread over its head like an umbrella and was chewing on a nut, eyeing them suspiciously. Suddenly it dropped its tail, spread leathery bat-wings, and flew off squawking.

'I fear this forest,' said Cautes. 'I feel it watching us. But that creature was eating a nut. Perhaps we could find its source.' They spread out for a little while, and soon Pike called, laughing, and they followed the sound of his voice and saw that he was standing by a bush laden with nuts. They picked as many as they could carry, filling their mouths and pockets.

'The leaves of the nutbush are full of moisture,' said Pike. 'Look!' He bit into one, and licked his lips; the rest followed suit.

Little though it was, it gave them energy to continue.

'What do you think those insect creatures were?' asked Simon.

'I do not know,' replied Cautes. 'I have been thinking, searching in my mind for anything I might have seen or heard in my time in the realm, or in your world, or in the kingdom. But nothing comes close. They may be inhabitants of this place – a place I do not know – or they may be set here by the Broken King to prevent anyone from aiding the goddess. It is the latter that I fear – for what else might he have set in place? How far do his revenges reach?'

The trees in the forest were growing more thickly together, so that soon the friends were scrambling over roots, and squeezing between gnarly boles, their bark whorled and scarred. It felt as if the forest itself was pushing inwards, impeding their progress, and with that sense came a mental heaviness that dulled their thoughts.

Soon they had each become a system of actions: step, pull, squeeze; step, pull, squeeze.

It was Johnny who spoke what they were all thinking. 'I can't go on like this,' he said. 'How much further is it?' *Wouldn't it be better*, he wanted to say, *to just sit here and let these trees engulf us?*

Pike said, 'We have to keep going,' but his voice was weak.

'We must keep going,' agreed Cautes, but even he was faltering.

'Come on, Johnny,' said Flora, her voice unexpectedly bright. 'We've got this far.'

'It's all because of you!' answered Johnny savagely. 'If you hadn't done this, called the Broken King, I'd –'

'Be a wreck, lying on your stupid bed!' shouted Flora hotly, and tears ran down her cheeks.

'And that would be better than this!' replied Johnny. He sank down into the roots of a tree. 'Leave me here. I want to disappear. I want to become part of this forest, and do nothing but drink the sun all day.'

Flora stared at him, and could not form the words to express her meaning.

'You . . . you . . . *idiot*.' It was the strongest insult she could think of. 'You would let the worlds die? You would die yourself?'

'Oh, why not?' said Johnny. 'What is there to live for, anyway?'

Flora, speechless with rage, simply stuttered a half-sob, half-cry, when Cautes let out an exclamation.

'Come on,' he said. 'I think we're here.'

He didn't say what it was, but waited till they

had all climbed over the thick branch that lay in the way, Johnny coming last and grudgingly.

There, opening up in front of them like a gaping, monstrous mouth, was a vast pit, black and sooty and flickering with small fires. Far down in the centre of it was the unmistakeable shape of the bound mare.

There was a groaning sound, distant yet terrible, and Cautes shuddered. 'I can feel her pain,' he said. 'How could Selenus have done such a thing?'

'We have to rescue her immediately!' said Simon. 'There doesn't seem to be anything guarding her. Come on, let's go!'

'That is what's worrying me,' said Cautes, holding him back from rushing down the slope of the pit. 'I would say let's do a reconnaissance, but I don't think that we should split up.'

'Never a good idea,' muttered Flora. 'Given a chance of splitting up to look round a fiery pit where anything might be lurking, or staying together, I think most people would opt for the latter.'

Once more Simon felt a smile forming on his lips, and he looked gratefully at Flora.

The mare, they could see, was bound tightly, as she had been in Simon's vision. Round her the black pit roared and fumed. Pike experimentally threw a pebble into it. The pebble fizzled, the dark mulch made a loud gulping noise, and sucked it from sight.

Looking closer, they could see the mare was on a little island of solid ground, about a hundred paces down from them, and all around her was a wasteland of sulphurous quicksand. As they looked, a piece of the edge of the island crumbled and fell into the quagmire. The mare whinnied – a terrible, almost human, sound.

'What will happen if she . . . goes?' asked Simon.

'Can't you feel it?' answered Cautes. 'I feel it, all the time. Everything is trembling. It will be as if a third of the universe is ripped out.'

'How do we get to her?' said Flora.

'Look around,' said Pike. 'Is there anything we can use as a bridge?'

They scanned the land about them, the black forest behind them.

'Oh!' said Flora. 'The forest! Could we cut down a tree and lay it over the pit?'

Cautes pinched the bridge of his nose in thought. 'We need to rest it on the edge, so that it doesn't touch the surface of the pit, or it will be pulled down and destroyed. And it needs to be wide enough to allow the mare to cross.'

The mare whinnied once more, and strafed against her bonds.

'How on earth are we going to do that?' said Johnny shakily, sitting down, his back against a tree.

'The horn and the sunsword,' said Pike. 'They still work a little. Maybe we can make a pile of stones and rest the end of the trunk on it on this side, and then lower the trunk down to the island?'

The flames burned below them as Cautes considered it, his fine, handsome features dotted with soot, his golden hair dishevelled. 'It's the only thing we can do,' he said. 'Let's do it.'

Flora and Cautes started piling up stones into a small bank; Johnny watched blankly as the rest of them turned back to the forest. He did not want to do anything. He didn't care any more. What was the point? Everything he'd learned so far had been overturned. He pinched the fleshy part of his arms, wishing the whole thing had never happened, and buried his face in his knees.

The tall trees rustled and swayed and loomed menacingly, as if they knew what was going to happen. Simon pushed aside the thought that they might be maliciously animated. *They are just trees*, he tried to convince himself.

He studied the nearest ones, thick-trunked and gnarly. The bridge needed to be about as wide as his arm span, so that the mare could walk on it. He spotted one, and lifted up the hunting horn. For a moment he thought he sensed some movement in the forest – eyes watching him, bright and interested – but the sensation vanished almost as soon as it had begun.

Settling the rim of the horn on his lips, he recalled the instructions that Lavinia, the Lady of the Stag, had given him. He would need to blow only a little, but then the horn was not so powerful here as it was in the kingdom, so he blew harder than he had done when he'd split the rocks by the Hall of the Sundering.

The horn's note was muffled, and nothing happened. He shot a worried glance at Pike, and then tried once more, harder.

This time, a crack appeared in the bole of the tree.

Simon and Pike ran towards it and stood on the side away from the pit, and began pushing with as much power as they could gather.

The tree moaned alarmingly, and then gave one final, crackling shriek, before toppling to the ground.

Pike and Simon took either end, and Cautes and Flora came to help. At Cautes's command, they lifted, and, half dragging, half carrying it, they managed to get the trunk to the edge of the pit.

They heaved the severed trunk on to the pile of stones, leaving enough room to swing it round and down.

'One of us will have to go across it to release her,' said Cautes. 'I would go . . .'

'You can't,' said Flora, looking at his bound leg.

'I am healing fast,' said Cautes, but he winced as he said it.

'Those bonds will need more than a knife to loosen,' said Simon, remembering his vision.

'The sunsword,' said Flora resolutely. 'I'll do it. I'm lighter than any of you, anyway.'

'Simon, Cautes and I will hold the base of the tree,' said Pike, 'and we'll lever it down.'

They did so, carefully, gritting their teeth, sweat pooling on their foreheads and under their armpits. There was a horrible moment when Pike slipped and almost lost his grip, and was about to fall into the pit. But he righted himself, and they landed the tip of the tree on the island. The tree's trunk was clear of the pit's surface, but some of the branches were dangling dangerously close to being sucked in.

Pike took hold of the base, and Simon joined him, with Cautes on his other side. Down below the fires popped and spat, and the mare whinnied sharply.

Flora looked at Johnny, but he was avoiding her gaze entirely. Instead, Simon squeezed her shoulder with his left hand. Flora looked like she was about to approach her brother, then she changed her mind.

She considered the descent. She could, she thought, go down on her hands and knees, facing the others. It was about a hundred paces, maybe a little more, but across that black and burning expanse the island seemed almost unreachable.

Gritting her teeth, she unsheathed the sunsword. She felt the familiar buzzing at the back of her mind, weak and faint; the blade glowed dimly.

She tested it on one of the down-hanging branches. It sliced through neatly with a satisfying sound, and the branch fell into the pit, where it took flame instantly, turning to ash in seconds.

Simon said, 'Are you sure you want to do this?'

Flora nodded. The sunsword, though weak, still retained some of its force, and again she felt its voice was calling to her, reassuring her, giving her strength.

She straddled the end of the trunk, re-sheathed

the sunsword, then began, inch by inch, to make the descent.

The tree trunk wavered ever so slightly underneath her. Not far away were the faces of her friends: Cautes, his golden hair ruffled and lank; Simon, gazing at her with a worried look in his eyes; Pike, determined, his arm pressed to his chest in a gesture of comradeship.

There was no sign of her brother.

Nobody said anything, and she was obscurely thankful for this. If they'd called out, she might have broken down and refused to go.

Carefully, she began shinning down the trunk, peering at her feet, testing for toeholds. The bark was rough under her fingers.

As she shuffled down, she felt an unpleasant sensation on her right hand. She looked up to see a black scorpion crawling out of the trunk and across it. It had a huge, dangerous-looking stinger rising from its back. She froze and stared at it, hardly daring to breath.

It clicked, agonisingly slowly, over her knuckles. As soon as it had reached the bark she brushed it away sharply with her wrist, and it fell into the pit, burning up instantly.

Soon her friends were almost indistinguishable in the smoky fumes. For a brief, horrifying moment, they appeared to be insubstantial, as if their solid forms had vanished and they'd been replaced with shadows.

Panicking for a second, Flora called up to them. 'Are you there?'

A second later, though she felt it as if a great amount of time had passed, she heard an answering shout from Simon. 'Keep going! You can do it!'

His voice gave her new purpose. The illusion faded. They were up there after all. She continued downwards, knees scraping against the bark, her palms now blackened and torn.

The smoky fumes from the pit were strong, and she tried not to breathe them in too deeply, though she could not stop them stinging her eyes.

She was now midway. Above her, that ghostly collection of faces. Directly below her, the pit. And at the end of the trunk, danger.

Summoning up her courage, she composed herself, and clambered the rest of the way like a squirrel, landing squarely on the island. She thought she heard a muffled shout but could not now make out any figures above her at all. The trunk seemed to disappear into the smoke.

The sound of a snort made her turn round. There was the mare. She was entirely tied up in a thin rope.

Flora stepped gingerly forwards, and kept her movements slow and gentle.

'There now,' she said. 'I've come to help you.'

The mare was grey, beautiful, like a racehorse. She snorted, her eyes rolling wildly into the back of her skull, and she flicked her tail.

Flora, panting slightly, took the sunsword from its sheath and slowly approached the mare. She stretched out the tip of the sword and slid it under the rope where it touched the mare's neck, and then pulled it upwards in a sharp swift movement.

She was not prepared for what happened next.

The mare screamed, a human sound, almost unbearable. The rope came away, but with it a strip of the mare's flesh. Flora could see the long bloody gash that it left behind.

The mare, spooked and hurt, screamed again, shifting against its bonds, and Flora dropped the rope, which sealed itself back on to the mare, leaving the wound open.

Flora's heart filled with pity. How could she save this magnificent beast? The mare's gorgeous, liquid eyes stared at Flora, full of wild pain.

Flora turned back to the tree trunk, and yelled up into the gloom. But there was no reply, no shout of encouragement. The wind billowed, blowing fumes into her nostrils, and she coughed, bent over for a second, her eyes smarting.

Raising herself, she considered the situation. There was the mare, trapped and frightened. Any attempt to free her from those bonds would only harm her further. She was on an island, alone, surrounded by a tarry, fuming, burning pit.

She caught the mare's eye, and she said, 'You are a goddess, and I have come to help you. But I don't know what to do. I don't know what to do. I'm scared . . .' She fell to her knees.

I don't know what to do, she said again, but she didn't know if she was saying it or thinking it now, and it seemed to become part of everything around her, the island, the smoke, the fumes, the goddess. *What is the point?* she thought. *Something will destroy us. We will be nothing, soon enough. I can't free the mare any more than I can free myself.*

From somewhere came a whisper. Was it the sunsword? No, it was different. It was a voice, calm and womanly, and it said, 'You do. You do.'

Flora pushed herself upwards. The mare was

gazing at her, and she suddenly felt a connection, as if her mind had opened up and she was given access to some terrible, strange secret. The mare was giving her the answer, showing her what to do.

She saw herself mired in a scarlet flood, and weeping. 'No,' said Flora. 'I can't do it.'

The mare whinnied, but gently.

Flora knew what she would have to do. The message was unmistakeable. It came from the mare herself.

Steeling herself, she stood, and went to the side of the mare, and said, 'I am sorry.'

And then, with the tip of the sunsword, she unpicked the rope, and pulled.

Flora deafened her ears to the mare's cries. She pulled and pulled, and the rope came off, tearing with it chunks of the mare.

As she pulled, she wept, and the mare screamed. Her eyes were blinded with tears and fumes, and soon she was dripping with blood. But still she pulled.

Standing by the base of the fallen tree, the others listened in horror.

They couldn't see anything through the gloom, but they could hear the screams, which seemed to pierce through the shell that had grown around Johnny, because he suddenly started and stared at them as if he had just woken up.

'My sister!' Johnny said. 'Where's my sister?'

'She's down there,' said Pike, pointing.

'You let her go down there? Is that her screaming?'

'I don't know,' said Pike, at a loss, as Johnny grabbed him fiercely.

'What are you doing?' shouted Simon.

'I have to go down there.' Johnny let Pike go and peered over the edge.

'No,' said Cautes. 'Wait. I feel something.'

'What if she's hurt?' yelled Johnny.

The screams stopped, and there was a moment of silence, a moment which expanded and became eternity.

And then the base of the trunk shook.

'She's on it!' cried Johnny, over the edge of the pit. 'Flora! Flora, can you hear me?'

They held the trunk still, all gazing intently through the fumes.

Soon they saw a familiar figure, with a sword at its belt, crawling up the tree trunk. It was slightly misshapen.

'Are you hurt? Flora, are you hurt?'

She did not answer for a second or two. Her shape became clearer. Now it seemed that she was hunched over, cradling something in her right arm.

'Come on, then,' came her voice, distant and weary, but with a touch of that humour that they all knew. 'Someone help me!'

Johnny eagerly reached down, and took the proffered bundle, as Flora emerged, face blackened, shaking, and then the rest of them were hauling her up until she stood at their side, begrimed and battered, and they hugged her until she said, 'The mare!'

But the mare was not behind her. It was nowhere to be seen.

Johnny lifted up the bundle. It was his leather jacket, but something was moving beneath it. He uncovered what was in it, gasped, then gently handed it to Flora.

Inside, slick, wet and shaking, was a foal.

A beautiful, perfect, newborn foal.

Chapter Fourteen

THE
TRAPPED EAGLE

T HE FUMES OF the burning pit soaked the air,
seeping into the travellers' lungs and clinging
to their skin. As they trudged away from it, Johnny
supported Flora, whilst Cautes hobbled on his
crutch. Pike strode on further ahead to scout out
the way, so Simon carried the foal.

'She's so small,' said Simon. 'What can she do?'

'Her being free is enough,' replied Cautes. 'She
will grow in strength, and her strength will aid the
repairing of the worlds.'

Simon turned his attention back to the sleeping
foal. He had never come so close to such a young

animal before. Carefully, he wrapped it in his jumper, and made a sling out of the arms, which he tied around his neck. She lay curled up for the most part, her absurdly long legs concertinaed underneath her. Her tiny body was gently fluttering with breaths, her delicate eyelashes flickering.

He felt a great rush of tenderness towards the little creature, and he found himself whispering nonsense to her. She woke, and made a whimpering noise. Simon fed a leaf to her, and she chewed on it steadily.

The others kept quiet, walking knotted together in a small group around Simon, instinctively protecting the foal.

After they had walked for about half an hour, and the sun was hovering a quarter of the way above the horizon, they reached the brow of a hill from where they could see down into a plain below them. The air was clear. Cautes looked around and said, 'Here's as good a place as any.' There was a small copse where they could sit in shelter, whilst still being able to see if anything was coming from any side. Pike stood at the edge of the group, looking out, shading his eyes.

Simon gently laid down the still-sleeping foal, and then settled on his back beside her and tried to shut his eyes. He knew he would not be able to sleep, but just for a moment he wanted only to feel the foal's soft coat against his skin, and her gentle, regular breathing.

He tried to steady his mind, and found that he was breathing in time with the foal. His eyes closed, and a feeling of weary bliss spread through him. He sensed the others settling around him, and felt peace for the first time in ages.

Flora was snuggling into the arms of her brother, who was holding her carefully, her head buried into his shoulder. They hadn't exchanged a word since she'd come back from the pit, but it was clear that Johnny had been jolted by what had happened to her.

'I'm sorry,' he said to them all. 'My mind . . . it just folded in on itself. I felt a huge block and I couldn't do anything.'

'Do not fear,' said Pike. 'We have all faced such moments.' He squeezed Johnny's shoulder.

Cautes was keeping watch back the way they'd come, whilst Pike looked out ahead over the plain. Battered and tired though they were, the air had lightened, and they sat in silence listening to the wind.

As Simon rested, eyes closed, he heard a voice,

gentle, whispering to him. And then the copse and his friends and the foal fell away from him, and he was running in a field, the air rushing through his hair, and he wasn't Simon at all – he was a horse.

He was galloping, rushing for the sheer joy of it, his muscles exulting in the movement.

A grey mare was waiting at the crest of a hill, her head turned towards him, and joyfully he ran towards her. The mare, whinnying, set off too, and he was chasing her now across a broad green plain, long grasses tickling his knees, the sun blazing down upon them and the fresh scent of spring in his nostrils.

He soon caught up with the mare, and she ran alongside him for a second or two, her eyes shining and lustrous, then she put on more speed and went ahead. Simon spurred himself.

He knew, though, that he would never be able to catch up with her. She was so fast and light it was as if she flew. She was like a shadow, or a piece of thistledown floating in the wind.

Soon the mare stopped at the top of another hill, and Simon came thundering up to her side. She turned her head towards the plain below.

There was a small encampment, winking with

light and movement. It was as if Simon was given special sight, as suddenly he could see among the tents. He saw men fighting and playing dice; soldiers polishing armour.

Standards and pennants with the sign of an eagle upon them fluttered in the breeze. He did not have time to wonder what the place was, or who the men were, as he saw a terrible, sad sight.

Chained to a roost behind a large chair, on which a general was sitting and drinking from a goblet of wine, was an eagle. She hobbled awkwardly from side to side. Those ropes, the same terrible thin ropes that had bound the mare, were cutting into her feathers.

That's the eagle, thought Simon, *the part of the goddess we must rescue next. But she is guarded by all those men . . .* He turned to the mare, and tried to communicate with her, ask her where they were, how this might be achieved.

But the mare was already galloping away, a white streak against the dark green grasses. Simon tried to run after her but he couldn't; his legs were too short, too slow, and he looked down to see that he was no longer a horse, but back in his human form.

Someone was shaking his shoulder, and he

opened his eyes to see Flora's dirty face smiling down at him. Pike was already striding down the hill.

'Come on,' she said. 'We've got to move on. Cautes has heard something close by.'

The meaning of his vision hit Simon. The goddess had been showing him the way to the eagle. 'I know where to go. There's a military camp, by a hill, in that direction,' Simon said, pointing. 'We must go there.' He explained his vision briefly to the others. Cautes nodded, and they gathered their things, and set off towards the sun.

After they'd left, there was silence for a few minutes where they'd camped, then a bush stirred, and Cygnet and Anna came out.

Cygnet was tired. The fumes from the pit had made him choke. Anna was beginning to annoy him, too.

'I want to talk to them now!' she said again. 'Why can't we join up with them?'

'All in good time,' said Cygnet. 'We are still not sure if we can trust them. They may not be who we think they are. Nothing is what it seems in this place. It's best to wait and see.'

'All right then,' said Anna. 'Come on, let's go!'

Anna set off after the little group, and Cygnet, sighing, followed.

'Who are they?' said Pike, indicating the soldiers below them, as they stood on the hill that Simon had seen in his vision. 'Where are they from?'

They'd been walking at a steady pace for about half the day. The foal had grown no heavier in Simon's arms; she felt like a feather, so light and slender was she. Sometimes he would forget she was there, until a small movement of her legs kicking into his chest would remind him.

He also found himself wondering about Anna. How was she, back in the temple, with Mithras and Arion? She would be all right, he tried to convince himself.

'I don't know who these soldiers are,' said Cautes, bringing Simon back to the present. 'They don't look like a part of this world. There's nothing here to attack, nothing to guard. They're not meant to be here.'

'Like that beast in the mountain pass?' said Flora.

'Yes,' said Cautes. 'Perhaps they've slipped in by accident. We should scout them out before we do anything.'

There was a path that wound down the hill, providing ample cover with bushes and trees and rocks. The encampment was made up of about fifty tents, a larger one in the middle. Fires were burning, and soldiers went about their affairs throughout the camp. The faint sound of shouting came on the breeze.

'I want to do it,' said Johnny.

Cautes looked at him levelly for a second, then nodded. 'All right. Keep to the shadows and don't let them see you.'

Johnny assented. He glanced at Flora. 'I won't be long,' he said.

Flora hugged him deeply. 'Don't . . .' She was about to tell him not to do anything stupid, but looking at her brother she realised how much had changed. He wanted to help. He had a look in his eyes she hadn't seen for a long time, since she'd been a little girl and he'd encourage her to climb trees. 'Don't get hurt,' she said instead.

Johnny set off, leaving the others discreetly watching from the brow of the hill. Johnny had been pinching himself resolutely since they'd arrived in this world. It couldn't be a hallucination, he knew; it was too involved, too ordered. He also knew that you could stop hallucinations if you tried, but however hard he told himself that what he was seeing wasn't real, everything was still there when he opened his eyes.

And his sister, Flora, was proof of it too. She'd changed. She wasn't a little girl any more. She was strong and brave, and she knew how to use a sword in battle. It made him feel inadequate. So he was going to do this, scout out this camp, help however he could.

The descent wasn't that steep, and he found that if he half walked, half crawled, he could easily keep out of sight. At one point he startled something in the bushes, and watched as a rabbit sprinted away, its little white scut bobbing up and down. He held his breath, stayed still for a few moments, but there was no shout of surprise from the camp.

When he reached the bottom of the hill, there was empty flat ground between him and the nearest tent. He couldn't see anyone in the vicinity, no guards posted along the perimeter, but there was a disturbance in the middle of the camp – men shouting and roaring.

He dashed across the open space, and hid behind the nearest tent. It was made of leather and smelled very potent. The scent of roasting meat also filled the air; some rabbits hadn't been lucky.

Creeping zig-zag fashion from one tent to another, Johnny soon neared the centre of the camp.

There was a heated discussion going on. Some soldiers were talking amongst themselves, gesturing expansively, whilst a man – obviously their commander, judging by the way the others deferred to him – looked on. A taller man in a plain brown tunic was at the commander's side, gazing at everything expressionlessly. He had a hollow face and piercing dark eyes.

Johnny couldn't understand what they were saying. He could catch some words. *Periculo*, was that? It stirred something in his brain, from long ago when he was a small boy. *Caesar* . . . He knew what that meant.

Then it struck him. The eagles on the standards, the leather tents . . . There were long red shields on the ground, and the soldiers' leather sandals looked familiar, too.

These were Romans, he realised. Romans, from Earth's past. *How did they end up here?* he wondered. He crept forwards to see if he could catch any more of what they were saying.

The commander was a hefty-looking man with a long nose and cropped black hair. He wore a bronze breastplate but was otherwise unprepared for battle of any sort. He seemed untroubled by what was going on among his men. A goblet hung from his right hand, and he would occasionally sip from it.

'*Haruspex*,' Johnny heard someone say. The taller man replied, and another heated argument broke out between the men.

'*Dei id volunt!*' one of the soldiers shouted. The taller man nodded, and spread his palms out wide, whilst the commander remained impassive.

The soldiers parted. Then a younger one appeared, not much older than Johnny. He was leading a roe deer on a rope. She was young and trembling, her neck twitching about, left to right and back again, her eyes shining with fear.

The soldier took her up to the commander and the tall man, and the two conversed for a second. The commander gave a sign of assent, and drained his goblet. Then the tall man turned round and removed a long knife from a bag on a table behind him. *He must be the priest*, thought Johnny.

Johnny realised what they were about to do. They were going to kill the deer. Why, he didn't know – a sacrifice, perhaps, to the gods.

And something about the deer, its frightened, liquid eyes, meant that he couldn't stand it happening.

It was all too much. Everything that he'd seen, everything that he'd done so far, all rolled up into an unbearable mass, pushing down on him. He had to stop this one thing. Everything else was out of his control.

Without really thinking about what he was doing, Johnny ran out into the open, shouting all the while, and threw himself at the tall man, knocking him over. Johnny righted himself, took the rope from the soldier, and stood in front of the deer.

'No!' he shouted. 'You won't do it!'

Panting, he looked about at the ring of soldiers, all confused and uncertain, and at the commander, at the priest who was staring at him intently.

'*Incolane huius loci es?*' said the tall man. '*Autne deus es?*' He sounded a little fearful.

Johnny thought hard back to hazy memories of school. *Deus.* That meant *god*, didn't it? *Es* sounded like *is*. Was the man asking him if he was a god?

Johnny was at a loss. 'I don't know what you're saying!' he stuttered. '*Parlez-vous . . . er . . .*'

'*Non deus est,*' snarled the priest. '*Hostis!*'

As the soldiers closed in on him, he realised what a stupid thing he'd done. The deer, frightened, strained at the rope, and he let it go. Startled, it hared off among the tents, and was gone before any of the soldiers could so much as shoot an arrow after it.

'*Eum neca!*' shouted the tall man.

Johnny may not have known much Latin, but he could understand people well enough, and there was no mistaking the fire in the priest's eyes, or what he was saying.

Kill him.

Chapter Fifteen

LEGIONARIES

T HE SKY ABOVE the group of travellers was grey, and it looked as if at any moment a fine mizzle might fall. Flora had recovered from her ordeal in the pit now, and was looking about the scene with renewed interest, lit as it was with weak sunshine. Pike was keeping watch at the back for any sign of movement, whilst Simon carefully tended to the foal. He was feeding her droplets of water from his finger, and enjoying the lapping of her lips on his skin.

They were startled by a rustling noise, and suddenly, like a catapulted shot, a deer raced past them, vanishing beyond them down the hill.

'Tell me why that doesn't seem like a good thing,' said Flora.

They waited for a little while longer. Nothing more stirred out of the bushes or scrub, not even a rabbit. Pike whistled through his teeth, and practised thrusts with his sword.

'How long has Johnny been gone?' asked Flora eventually.

They couldn't see much activity in the camp below, and chewed on the nutbush leaves reflectively.

Simon stroked the foal, feeling her little heart beat, her whole frame shaking. *How strange*, he thought, *that I am holding this creature. She is divine, torn from forces beyond my understanding. And yet at the same time she is totally powerless. For the moment, at least.* He stroked the foal's forehead. She whinnied in response, a little gentle sound that touched his heart.

Flora began to get restless. She was fiddling with the hilt of her sunsword, pulling it in and out of its sheath, so that the dim light winked on and off a few times before Cautes warned her to stop, in case it attracted attention.

'Shouldn't we go down after him? He's been gone ages!' she said.

'I agree,' added Pike levelly.

Cautes thought for a second, then nodded. 'We shall. But we will go carefully, making signs of peace. Simon, you go first, carrying the foal, with Flora. Then they shall see that we mean no harm. I will go next with Pike, and we will hold our weapons hilt outwards. They will not harm three young people and a wounded man.'

'What if they don't think like you and attack us?' said Flora in an undertone.

'Then we have weapons to hand, and I still have some energy left.'

Slowly, they moved down the hill in full view. There was nobody watching from the camp, however, and they made it right amongst the tents without being challenged or with anyone seeing them.

As they approached, they saw that all of the four or five hundred soldiers were standing in a square around a small group of figures.

Flora recognised one of them immediately. 'Oh my God – it's Johnny!'

He was tied up, and being held in between two soldiers. The priest was holding his arms out wide and uttering incantations to the sky, brandishing a long, gleaming knife in his right hand.

The little group of friends rushed forwards. 'Stop!' shouted Flora, recklessly pushing her way through the soldiers. 'You have to stop! Don't kill him!'

The priest, seeing Flora's strange clothes and look of determination, looked frightened, and when Cautes and Simon appeared too, he trembled at Cautes's blond radiance. The soldiers made no movement, waiting for a signal from their leader.

The commander put down his goblet, and was about to say something when Cautes stepped forwards, still glowing gently with the energy of the Golden Realm. He spoke out loud, his voice rich and warm, '*Mihi nomen Cautes est – comes Mithrae sum.*' His unearthly voice exuded power and rolled around the camp, and the startled soldiers ceased their chattering and jostling, and stood as still as rabbits caught in an unexpected light.

The priest bent his head, and then, placing the knife down on the ground, he knelt and prayed loudly. The soldiers released Johnny, and he rushed towards Flora, embracing her closely.

The commander, taking his cue from the priest, knelt too, slightly more cumbersomely, and all the men followed suit in a clattering of armour.

Simon could make out one word from the jumble of what they were saying.

'Mithras . . . Mithras . . .'

He remembered. Of course. Mithras! Roman soldiers worshipped him as a sun god.

He caught Flora's eye. She made a face at him, and he smiled back. Pike took his arm and whispered, 'That's it! We've almost got the eagle now.'

The little foal in Simon's arms was stirring, feeling the presence of her sibling.

Cautes, joyful, shouted something in Latin, and the soldiers stood up, delight suffusing their faces as the priest gabbled at him.

'They think I've come to rescue them,' said Cautes, translating what the priest was saying.

Within a few minutes, the priest and the commander had ushered them into the large tent in the middle of the encampment. The other soldiers remained outside, talking amongst themselves, the wonder evident in their voices.

Simon caught the word *domum* and he knew what that meant. They wanted to go home. *Just like us*, thought Simon ruefully.

Inside the tent it was cool and shadowy. The

commander indicated to them that they should sit on the long couches that stood on either side of the tent, which they did, gratefully.

The foal in Simon's arms stirred, and began to whicker gently. A soft cry came in answer from the other side of the room, with a flutter of movement. Through the gloom a sad sight became clear.

'That's the eagle!' exclaimed Simon. He released the foal, pouring her on to the ground, and she tottered over to where the eagle was tethered and bound, and began to reach up and nuzzle it.

The reaction of the soldiers could not have been more surprising. The commander drew his sword, and the priest placed himself in front of the eagle and started babbling loudly in Latin. Pike pulled out his sword too, but Cautes shushed him, and Pike resheathed it reluctantly.

'What are they saying?' asked Simon as the foal pushed her little nose past the priest and up to the eagle.

'They are lost and confused,' said Cautes, easily interpreting. 'The commander is called Gaius Fabius, and the tall man is a priest, Marcus Caelius. They do not know how long they have been here, but they reckon by the sun about three days. They were setting up camp in a forest somewhere called Germania, and then they felt a terrible rushing noise, and everything went black. When it passed, they were here.'

'Time is all scrunched up,' said Johnny. 'They're from our past, but they're in our present.'

'It happens,' said Cautes. 'The Centre of the Worlds doesn't really exist in normal time, anyway. They realised something was really wrong,' Cautes continued, 'when none of the scouts they'd sent out in Germania returned. About half of the legion vanished – from their point of view, anyway. Imagine what the others at home thought. They sent out a few soldiers here, who came back terrified, talking of strange sights and monsters. They fear that they are in the Underworld. They found the eagle, guarded, they say, by a terrible creature. They defeated the monster, and they thought it was a sign that they would find a way home. They have not explored very far yet, but they do not want to give up the eagle.'

'They will not give the eagle even to you?' said Simon.

'The eagle is their standard – they believe that she belongs to them, and that harm will come to them if they release her. I don't know how to get them out of here,' said Cautes. 'They must have slipped in through a crack when the king's trap was sprung. If I can't offer them a way back, then they won't relinquish her.'

'We could overpower them,' said Pike. Flora nodded her assent. Simon looked a little more uncertain.

'With all those soldiers outside? We wouldn't stand a chance,' said Johnny.

'Unless we did it secretly,' said Pike. 'We could deceive them somehow . . .'

The eagle was ruffling her feathers, bending down to caress the foal's head with her beak. Marcus the priest was intoning something, a light shining in his eyes. The commander, Gaius, offered the point of his sword around at each of them; even when Cautes moved forwards, he did not flinch.

'Ask them what they want,' said Pike.

'Home. They want to go home,' replied Cautes.

'How can we get them home when we don't even know how to go home ourselves?' asked Flora.

'When the goddess is healed, she will send us home,' said Cautes. He thought for a moment. 'So let's take them with us. Tell them what we're going to do – they'll bring the eagle with them.' He explained the idea to Gaius.

The commander looked crestfallen, but Cautes seemed to be managing to reassure him. Then the commander came to a decision, and drew himself up, barking out a reply in his gruff tones.

'They will not come with us,' said Cautes, sighing. 'They wish to keep the eagle.'

'Let me at least release her bonds?' said Flora. 'She's in pain!'

Cautes and Marcus entered into conversation. 'You may release her,' Cautes translated, 'but she must remain chained to the post.'

'I don't think they will want to see it happening . . .' said Flora.

'The foal is with her. That means it will be easier,' assured Cautes.

So Flora tentatively went towards the eagle and the foal. Marcus and Gaius stood back to give her access, and Flora unsheathed the sunsword.

It was glowing more brightly now, and it lit up the eyes of the foal and the eagle, soft and sharp. The bonds around the eagle were like those that had been around the mare. Taking a deep breath, Flora carefully inserted the tip of the blade underneath where they crossed over the eagle's wings, and pulled the sunsword up.

The bond snapped straight in two, and as the rope came off, it tore with it the feathers and skin of the eagle. The Romans gasped, and Gaius made a run for Flora, but Cautes held him still. *'Mane!'* he shouted.

The old skin fell away, and the eagle, struggling, managed to spread her wings wide. She appeared now bald and red, a strange lizard-like being. Huge suddenly, she reared upwards, opening her mouth and letting out a noise that was half-song, half-caw.

Marcus and Gaius dropped to the ground, and Cautes bent his head. The eagle roared, more like a lion than a bird, and the foal whinnied and went up on her hind legs.

The two touched beak to nose, and there was a blinding flash of white light. The ground trembled; a rushing noise filled their ears.

Wild, strange joy rolled around the room, making everybody laugh out loud. Soldiers gripped each other, feeling the force of the power that emanated from their union.

When the light faded from their eyes, they saw that the eagle was now feathered – small and glossy, but whole. The foal nuzzled the eagle's cheek, and the eagle stroked her mane tenderly with a wingtip.

The two separated, the eagle settling back on to her perch, and the foal curling up around the bottom of the post.

Cautes went to the pair and bowed.

A female voice issued from them both. 'You have saved us. We thank you. But our sister lies dying. We still must rescue her.' They moved as one, rising upwards. 'We have only a little power without her. We must rest until we are all reunited.'

'It shall be so, my goddess,' said Cautes.

The foal reached up her head and breathed on Cautes's leg; he straightened immediately, and threw away his crutch. 'I thank you,' he said smiling.

Gaius marched out and roared an order to his men.

They left the foal and the eagle in the tent as they settled down to sleep, and went outside to see what was happening.

They watched the soldiers striking camp with incredible speed and efficiency. Gaius marched up to Cautes.

'He has seen enough,' translated Cautes. 'They are coming with us.'

Soon they were formed up in marching order, the commander facing them, and the priest at his side with the eagle clamped on his arm.

'I've always wanted to travel with a Roman army,' said Flora to her brother. Pike looked pleased, too, and was enjoying examining the weapons.

Simon leaned down to pick up the foal as she stepped outside, but she sprang away from him and bounded ahead, stopping to look behind. She gambolled onwards up a small hill, as if saying, '*Follow me! Follow me!*'

Onwards they marched, a miniature army, a ragtag band, following a foal and carrying an eagle: a scattered band of Romans cast out of their time and space; Cautes, the supporter of a demi-god; Pike, the newly made knight; Johnny, a dreamy philosopher; and Simon and Flora, walking side by side, Flora humming *Jerusalem* under her breath, and Simon feeling resolution for battle forming in his chest.

Though they did not know what they might face, they were proud and strong, and as they marched, the Romans began to sing, feet pounding the grass, their voices echoing into the sky.

Chapter Sixteen

THE

DUEL

THEY MARCHED FOR half a day, following the foal, which pranced always ahead. They went over hilly, scrubby countryside, dotted with long grasses, insects fluttering and buzzing among them. In the early dusk, as the light began to fade, they came to the edge of a lake that stretched, silvery and cool, into the far distance. The foal stopped at the edge of it, and settled down.

Marcus the priest set up the perch for the eagle, and placed her reverently upon it. The eagle shook herself, her sharp eyes gazing everywhere, and then became as immobile as an idol.

With the same speed, the Romans set up their tents once more and soon had lit fires everywhere, around which they sat in groups, playing games with bones and dice, hawking and spitting and chuckling as if they'd never left Germania.

Gaius the commander insisted that the five companions join him in his tent, where they reclined on couches, resting uncomfortably on their elbows, and were served by two young soldiers. With Cautes acting as interpreter, Simon and Flora told Gaius as much of their story as they could. Surprisingly, Gaius did not have much trouble in believing it.

'He says stranger things happen in Rome,' said Cautes. 'Kings are enveloped in mist and taken up to heaven; ships change into nymphs.'

'I can believe that,' said Simon.

The commander then showed Simon and Pike to a tent they were to share, whilst Johnny and Flora had another; Cautes was given his own.

They went to sleep that night with a sense of electrical possibility in the air. Two parts of the goddess had been found, and there was a shifting in the order of things, as if a weight were coming back to where it ought to be.

But it was not over yet.

There was still the third part of the goddess to rescue.

As he slept, Simon dreamed once more.

Now he was strong, and so powerful. He could feel the sun in his bones, the wind in his sinews. The world crackled through his body. He was looking down on the camp from above, and below he saw a hunched figure on a post.

Instinctively, he soared down towards it, and saw that it was the eagle, who recognised him with a great cry, and they flew together into the air, the eagle going ahead, leading him over the great plain.

Below, everything was prey; anything that moved was within his grasp. He was an arrow of feathers, a machine made of instinct.

The eagle soared in a great loop and Simon followed, feeling the rush in his wings, his whole body tingling with a sense of place.

He knew the world; the world was in him.

Below them on the plain was a mass of moving things, and the eagle swooped low over their heads. Simon followed, eyes focusing in.

There was a woman, huge, snarling. She held a whip, her dress was bloody and unbound. A man was with her, encased in black armour, familiar and pale, sharpening his sword on a whetstone. Many black-armoured knights stood centred around a man who was dressed in a long red robe, his arms held aloft, a cruel smile on his lips, horns growing out of his head. Simon's heart quailed.

Behind the mass of figures was a great hill, crowned with a circle of standing stones – one with a vast black door in it, which opened to let the eagle and Simon in.

Through the door, unspeakably ancient, was a cave. In the cave, on a throne hewn out of stone, sat a woman. She was tall, bound in ropes, weak and weeping.

The goddess.

The pair of birds flew towards her, and the eagle touched her with her wings.

The goddess reached out to the eagle, turned to Simon and said, 'You who have come from the place in between. You have saved the mare and the eagle. Now you must come and rescue me, for the king's powers still hold me.'

The eagle screeched, and with a flap of her wings flew away, leaving Simon alone, gazing at the goddess.

*   *   *

When Simon woke, it was dawn, and he could smell roasting rabbit.

Flora poked her head through the flap of his tent. Pike groaned and rolled over. 'Come on, you two, I've been up for ages. These Romans are good swordsmen – they've been teaching me so many tricks!'

Simon sat up in bed. The vision he'd had the night before came back to him. The tall, horned man, his scarlet lips wide in a terrible smile, his cloak billowing about him. 'I saw him!' he said. 'He's here!'

'Who?' asked Flora. 'Hurry up, or all the rabbit will be gone.'

'You don't understand!' Simon's head swam with all the people and things he'd seen. The Broken King. The Knight of the Swan. But they were dead!

'He's here, and he's got a huge army, and he's guarding the goddess.'

'Who, Simon?' asked Flora, anxious now.

'Selenus,' he replied. 'The king. The Broken King himself.'

They were in the commander's tent. The door flaps fluttered gently in the breeze. The couches were laid out in attendance around Gaius's chair, the eagle on her stand next to him, and the foal peaceably at her feet.

The priest, Marcus, sat to one side, looking troubled. Johnny was shivering slightly and rubbing his arms; Flora was holding on to him, and whispering into his ear. Simon and Pike sat side by side on the couch, their weapons on their knees, gazing at Cautes.

Cautes was twisting his hands together, pacing up and down the tent. 'But the king died! I saw him! Are you sure about it?'

'The other visions from the goddess have been true,' said Simon.

Pike cleared his throat. 'I saw it too. Not as distinctly as Simon, but I definitely saw Selenus. I didn't want to tell anyone. I hoped it was just a dream. But I knew it wasn't.'

'It must be something else with his semblance – it can't be *him*,' said Cautes, stopping his pacing and turning to face Simon and Pike. 'What else did you see?'

Simon described the giant woman with her whip and her bloodied skirts. Turning to Gaius, Cautes translated. Gaius paled, and trembled, taking a huge draught of wine from his goblet. '*Magni dii . . . Bellona!*' he said. It took a lot to make this hardened soldier frightened – but what Cautes had told him had done so.

'Bellona,' said Cautes. 'A Roman war goddess.'

'Are we going to be fighting gods?' said Johnny sharply.

Cautes sighed. 'It looks like it,' he said.

At that point there was a commotion outside, and the voice of a little girl could be distinctly heard. Everyone went silent. The soldiers stopped sharpening their weapons. Gaius stood up and marched out of the tent. The others trooped after him.

The soldiers had formed into a ring, standing around a pair of figures. One was a tall, pale teenage boy in black armour. He had his arm around the other figure. And there was no mistaking who it was.

Anna. Too frightened to speak, she was red-faced and blubbing. Cygnet had a knife at her throat, and he was gripping her tightly with his left arm. He was looking about at the faces of all the soldiers, nervy and exhausted.

'Simon Goldhawk! Flora Williamson! The Knight of the Shark! Bring them to me!'

Flora loosened her hold of Johnny, and the three friends came slowly forwards and stood in a row before him.

Simon guessed who Cygnet was instantly. The

pale face, the black hair – there was no mistaking the family resemblance.

When Cygnet spoke, it was coolly. 'I am the son of the Knight of the Swan,' he said. 'I have followed you here to this strange world. I wanted to kill you in the temple! I wanted to get my revenge. You escaped then. I was going to wait, but this one got away from me and ran after you. I caught her, and I still want for vengeance!'

'Simon!' Anna called out suddenly, her voice strangulated and unnatural.

'Don't worry, Anna,' Simon replied, making himself sound as confident as possible. 'We'll get you out of this.' But he had no idea what to do.

'Do you know what it's like,' said Cygnet, 'to have the person you love the most taken from you?'

Simon nodded. 'I can guess,' he said quietly. 'It's why we came here, Flora and me. We . . . we lost our siblings.'

'They are alive still,' sneered Cygnet. 'My father is dead – because of you! He was a brave man – the most loyal of all the knights. And you caused his death!' His hand tightened on the knife and Anna squealed.

Simon edged forwards towards Cygnet, hands

outstretched in supplication. 'Please . . .' he said. 'Don't hurt her. She had nothing to do with it. She was just caught up in everything because of me. I have carried that guilt since before I came to the Silver Kingdom, since the messenger struck me by the sea.' He pointed to the welt on his cheek – fading now, but still clear. 'Since the day she was taken there isn't a moment when I don't feel it.'

'Nor me,' said Flora, and exposed the welt on the back of her leg. She glanced sideways at Johnny, who squeezed her arm.

The muscles in Cygnet's face twitched, and his nostrils flared.

Simon took one step further.

'Come any closer, and I will slit her throat!' Cygnet spat fiercely.

Simon paused. All around them the soldiers watched, uncertain how to act. Cautes looked on, helpless. Above them the sun was bright, and there was a heavy breeze that made the leather tents flap. Silence fell, of a kind that feels as if it might form itself into a living creature and suck the life out of everything.

Something clicked in Simon's mind. When the Knight of the Swan had died there had been a locket around his neck. He put his hand into his pocket, and felt it there. He drew it out slowly. It caught the light and glistened.

'This was your father's,' said Simon gently. 'You must take it.'

It was the wrong thing to do. Cygnet became visibly agitated, his grip around Anna tightening. 'Where did you get that?' he snarled.

'I . . .' Wrong-footed, Simon stumbled on his words.

'You took it from my father's corpse! You tore it from his lifeless body! Plunderer! Thief!'

'It's yours,' said Simon. 'Forgive me, please. Just, please – let Anna go.'

'She should die too!' shouted Cygnet. 'She should die, so that you know how it feels.' A change came over his face. 'That is what I will fight you for. The life of your sister.'

Anna screamed. Cautes murmured something to Marcus, and the commander looked up sharply.

'Simon! Don't do it!' urged Flora.

But Simon felt its force; he sensed Cygnet's vast loneliness, confusion and terror, and he shared it with him.

So Simon, feeling as if the world had focused on

him and Cygnet alone, nodded and bowed, placing the locket down by his feet. Cygnet, curling his lip, loosened his arm and lowered his knife. Anna collapsed on to the ground.

'You may tend to the girl,' said Cygnet. 'One of the soldiers is to look after her and the locket. Are you ready, sir?' he said, smiling his twisted smile.

As he looked at him, Simon remembered Cygnet's father, the Knight of the Swan: his handsome, cruel face; his strong hands around Simon's neck, and a rush of fear went through him.

'Sir,' said Simon. 'I am ready.'

'Are you sure about this?' Flora said to Simon quietly. 'I can –'

'You can fight better than me with the sunsword.' Simon finished her sentence for her. 'But I won't be using it. Just a normal one.' He snatched a look at Cygnet, now calm, testing his blade, and felt a pang of fear. A poem, unbidden, rose in his mind – something about a field in Flanders. *If I die here*, he thought, *then my parents will never even know I existed.* That had been what the messenger from the Golden Realm had promised. The thought filled him with inestimable horror. To counteract it, he picked up the sword and tried a few swings, thrusting and parrying and levelling it, feeling his muscles sing.

'He's wiry,' Pike was saying, 'strong and desperate. But I can see he's worn out and nervous. Look at his hands, they're trembling. You've got less strength than him, but you can make up for it by being quick. Try to give him the runaround and tire him out.'

Simon listened and nodded, as if in a daze.

Gaius had searched the soldiers and found one who was about the same size as Simon. He arrived, bearing his armour, and with an act of ceremonious solemnity, began to equip Simon.

The bronze breastplate was heavy. Gaius tied some leather guards on to Simon's forearms, and then placed a helmet on his head. It was hot and muffled inside the helmet. Simon wondered how he was meant to see effectively in it, and looked across at Cygnet, whose armour was plated and covered most of him.

Cygnet then began taking some of his armour off. 'We must fight equally,' he said. Roman armour was found for him.

As Gaius finished tightening straps around him, Simon felt unbearably hot and cumbersome.

'Let us begin. I presume you do not know the form?' said Cygnet.

'I do not,' answered Simon.

'We meet, bow, and then turn. We walk apart, ten paces, and face each other. And when the signal is given, we attack.'

'What is the signal?' asked Simon.

'The commander will drop his hand.'

'All right,' said Simon.

The rest of the camp had made a ring of spectators. Marcus was in a chair, flanked by Cautes and Johnny. Pike and Flora stood closer to the inside edge, whilst Anna was under guard. Simon looked towards the foal and the eagle, but the foal was simply gazing back at them, whilst the eagle's head was buried in her wing.

The fighters went through the form, then faced each other. The sun was hot and Simon's forehead was slippery with sweat. He tried to remember what Selena had taught him.

He kept his eye on Gaius, who slowly raised his hand. And then, all too soon, Gaius snapped it down, and a raging figure was haring towards him. Before Simon could react, Cygnet had made a swipe at him.

Simon just managed to parry the stroke. The force of the clash tingled through his body.

Cygnet circled him and came suddenly in from

behind, the blade glancing off the leather corselet Simon was wearing underneath the breastplate. It overbalanced him, and, unused to armour, he rocked.

Flora gasped in fear, but Cygnet simply wove his sword in the air, as if toying with Simon.

Simon planted himself firmly on the ground with both feet, and studied his opponent. The armour covered him well. His only hope was to knock him over and remove his helmet. And then . . . But he did not have time to consider further as Cygnet rushed towards him and the two began exchanging blows and fighting properly. Even though his mind was racing, Simon's body remembered what Selena had drilled into him.

Their swords rang together. Simon warded off a lunge, and managed to hack into Cygnet's flank, causing him to totter a little. Simon pressed the advantage, and aimed at Cygnet's knees, but Cygnet was too quick for him, darting away in a tight circle before coming back at him.

The pain was sharp and immediate, and Simon felt a wet stickiness in his side. The heat of it threatened to overwhelm him. At the edge of his vision he sensed Flora. She seemed to be saying something to him. Pike was shouting words of encouragement.

Cautes looked on in mute gravity.

Another blow rang, to the side of the head this time; it stunned him, and he teetered. His sword slipped out of his grip and he fell to the ground.

Cygnet stepped towards him and Simon tensed.

'I would not kill an unarmed man,' he said. 'Pick it up.'

Simon, shaking, slowly did so.

Facing Cygnet again, certainty dawned on him that he would not win. Cygnet was a tightly wound spring, fuelled by revenge, twisted into an uncontrollable tension. Simon batted away a stroke aimed at his neck and swung at Cygnet, but missed.

And then Cygnet had him. The strongest blow yet, and Simon teetered back and fell. With a swift movement Cygnet unstrapped his helmet, put his foot on Simon's chest and, exultant, held the sword with two hands and plunged it down at his neck.

What happened next, Simon and Cygnet could not really describe. It seemed at first that all sound drained from the world – and all sights, leaving Simon and Cygnet the only two people in it, the sword's point inches above Simon's neck.

Only the eagle on her perch, and the little foal remained.

The eagle reared up and stretched her wings, the foal in front of her, and for a brief moment it looked as if a woman was reaching out to them, arms outstretched. Then the eagle flew upwards, and the foal trotted towards them.

Cygnet dropped his sword. 'What is this?' he said. 'What are they doing?'

Simon, panting, lifted himself. 'The goddess . . .'

Cygnet's face twisted. He picked up his sword again, and aimed once more at Simon.

Simon blocked his blow, and the two became locked in a battle of strength, Simon pushing against Cygnet with all his might. The eagle swooped around them, her shadow passing over them; the foal ran in the opposite direction.

'Submit!' shouted Cygnet fiercely. But Simon could not. There was too much power inside him now, too much, and it all focused into his arm, and he pushed and pushed. Cygnet was weakening, his arm drooping. Simon, with one final exertion, shoved him back and pinned him down to the ground. Then, exhausted too, he relaxed, and rolled off Cygnet, lying on his back.

Cygnet stayed were he was, murder shining in his eyes. 'Why don't you kill me?' he said.

The eagle swooped back to her perch, the foal trotted to sit beneath her, and the world returned around them as it had been.

Nobody else had seen anything. One moment, Simon was all but dead; the next, Cygnet was on the ground, and Simon was getting steadily to his feet.

'Kill me! Do it!' Cygnet tore off his helmet and bared his neck. 'Finish it! What is there left for me?'

For a moment Simon pondered it. Some of the legionaries were cheering him on. He felt a surge of power rush through him, and the hatred he carried for the Knight of the Swan rose into his mind. He clutched his sword handle, and wavered.

But he knew that he could not. Slowly, he placed his sword upon the ground and shook his head. 'I did not kill your father, and I will not kill you.'

Cygnet howled with rage, and flung his helmet away from him. Tentatively, Simon moved towards him, took the locket from the soldier who'd been guarding it, and held it out to Cygnet. He did not say anything. Cygnet glared at it for a second, and then snatched it from him. He kept his eyes on the ground and Simon backed away.

Cautes signalled to two legionaries, and spoke to them in Latin, telling them to help Cygnet into a tent, and set a guard on him, and also to make sure that he had everything he needed. He went with them passively, limp like a doll, his face swollen with sorrow.

When he had gone inside, Simon sighed with relief, and Flora flung her arms around him and kissed him on the cheek. Anna appeared, delighted, then, as she saw the thunderous expression on his face, crestfallen, playing with the hem of her dress as Simon gripped her closely.

'What on earth did you think you were doing with him? Why didn't you stay at the temple?' said Simon after he'd buried his face in her shoulder.

Anna looked away, wriggling free of his grasp. 'I didn't want to be left behind with Mithras and Arion . . . and then I was all alone in that horrible dark place and that boy helped me follow you. He was nice, most of the time.'

Simon clutched his younger sister again as tears poured down her face. Then, whispering reassurance to her, he passed her to Cautes, who settled her in one of the tents.

'I thought you were a goner,' said Flora.

Pike hugged him too, and Johnny clapped him on the back. 'What happened?' asked Pike. 'Why didn't he kill you?'

'The goddess . . . She has some power still, even in those forms. She intervened . . . I think she gave me some of her energy – enough to overpower Cygnet, anyway.'

Simon released himself from the grip of his friends and went to the foal – who he realised was now more of a filly, being bigger and glossier than before – and the eagle, peering imperiously down from her perch, and bent low to them.

The filly nuzzled his cheek, and he felt her hot breath on him, and the eagle regarded him sideways, her ancient eye unblinking.

He stood for a moment, looking into that black pool, and he could not break away. Then the eagle ruffled her feathers, and Simon turned his gaze to the ground.

After they had rested, they marched once more, Cygnet deathly silent and under guard, the rest of them eagerly looking out for signs of the army Simon had seen.

Soon a tall circle of standing stones loomed above them from the crest of a hill. 'The home of the goddess,' said Cautes, spying it. 'We are near.' Not long after, they came to the brow of a hill opposite, and saw below them the enemy army.

From this distance it looked like row upon row of shining black beetles, and among them strode a woman, a giantess. Awed, Gaius looked to Cautes for guidance, who simply told them to set up camp.

'Who are those strange knights?' asked Johnny when they had finished, and Cautes was looking out below, shading his eyes.

'They are simulacra – replicas. They have substance, but it is important to remember that they are not what they seem to be. They are illusions, really. But that doesn't mean they can't kill us. And they are protecting the goddess – this is the king's last trap, and we must get through it.'

They set legionaries to watch, and Cautes and Gaius put up a table, drawing up plans for the battle ahead. The others lay, unsleeping, in their tents – Anna curled into Simon's side, Flora and Johnny together, Pike outside gazing at the army, testing his sword, flexing his limbs.

'Don't die, Simon,' said Anna quietly as the sun set. She held out the jewelled dagger Selena had given her.

'I won't,' answered Simon, and stroked her hair. 'You keep that.'

She nodded, tucking it back into its sheath, and slept, her little body moving gently up and down, and after a while Simon slept too.

Cautes and Gaius talked long into the night, and when dawn broke, they were still there, talking, and below them the great army of simulacra waited, black armour shining in the new sun, the goddess Bellona sharply cracking her whip.

Chapter Seventeen

BATTLE
BEGINS

THE EAGLE SWAM in the air towards the standing stones on the hill, beneath which was the cave where the goddess lived, and banked in a circle around it. Every time she tried to fly over the army, she was repelled, and forced away.

Steel and armour flashed in the light from the boiling sun. Bellona's huge shadow darkened the plain, forming a shadowy path to the home of the goddess. The giantess was twelve feet tall, and her hair rolled down her back in great waves as she cracked a giant whip, snarling and growling with the joy of the impending battle.

In her shadow, spread out in a vast formation, was an army. It was one thousand strong, and made up of knights in black armour, polishing their weapons, practising with their swords.

The clash and clamour of metal rang into the air, whilst royal hounds slunk around them, snatching at their heels and tussling over scraps.

In the middle of the army was a horned man, tall and unsmiling, seated on a horned horse, his scarlet cloak billowing around him. At his side stood another man, pale faced and black haired.

From where Simon watched with his friends and the army of Romans, gazing out over rank upon rank, it appeared as if all the knights looked the same.

'They *are* all the same,' said Cautes, as if reading Simon's mind. 'Identical. All replicants of an ideal knight. Brave and bold and strong. And, of course, deadly.'

He turned to confer with Gaius.

Bellona yawned, and cracked her whip in the air. The sound was like thunder.

Flora's face was set, and she whispered to Johnny as he hefted a sword under her direction. They went through a few more moves before Flora nodded in satisfaction, then jabbed at her brother. He wasn't quick enough, and the sword slipped by his flank. 'You see?' said Flora, pulling the blade back slowly. 'There are no rules. You just have to be faster than everyone else.'

'I still want to fight,' said Johnny. He was shivering, twitching at the prospect, but there was also a new resolve in his eyes.

'There are twice as many of them as us,' said Simon to Cautes. 'And the king . . . he's there!'

'It's not him,' Cautes reminded him, testing the weight of a javelin. 'But that doesn't mean he's not dangerous,' he continued levelly.

'What's the plan?' said Pike. He'd been scanning the rows of soldiers and was looking brisk and ready.

Gaius explained, and Cautes translated. Their only tactic was surprise. They were going to split up the legionaries into two vanguards. Marcus would lead the one on the left, which would aim to cut a line straight through to the replicant king. Simon and Johnny would march with him.

Gaius would lead the other, which would attack from the right. He would be followed by Flora with the sunsword, with Pike right beside her.

Cautes would direct the battle from above. Once

they'd made headway through the knights, then the first rank of the remaining legionaries would attack, coming straight down the hill into the front ranks, mopping up the knights so that the two incursions didn't get locked in and taken down from behind.

In reserve would be Cautes, and one more line of legionaries, ready to bring help to wherever most needed it.

Cautes said that the king had placed a shield around the goddesses' home which they could not break through; it was also preventing the foal and the eagle from taking their human forms and unleashing their full powers. Only when the replicant king was destroyed would the shield fall.

Anna was to remain in the commander's tent, with two legionaries guarding her; Cygnet was bound to a stake nearby, watched over by a single soldier, defeat visible in his every limb.

'We must get through to the cave of the goddess as soon as possible,' said Cautes. 'Once we are in there, we can reunite her three forms and all will be well. But first the army must be dealt with.'

'And Bellona,' mused Pike.

At her name Gaius muttered and closed his eyes briefly. '*Magni dii . . .*'

As if knowing that somewhere her name had been spoken, the giantess roared, something between a war cry and a shriek. The mass of black knights below banged their shields and their swords together in answer, so that the whole sky resounded with the noise.

Whether it struck fear into the heart of Cautes or not, he remained outwardly calm. It certainly struck fear into Simon's heart, and he gripped the hunting horn so tightly that his knuckles whitened.

'I've never fought like this before,' said Simon. 'I've only read about battles . . . I've never even dreamed of being in one.'

'Neither have I,' said Flora. 'But somehow I feel like I'm meant to be doing it. I wonder if it's the influence of the sunsword.'

'You seem to like all this more than I do,' said Simon.

'It's true.' Flora nodded. 'Though I wouldn't use the word *like* . . . More as if it feels right.' Her connection with the sunsword was buzzing; she heard its voice dimly at the back of her mind, giving her strength, encouraging her. She waved her sword in a series of loops, and Marcus said approvingly, '*Camillae similis est.*'

'What did he say?' asked Flora.

Cautes smiled. 'He says you are like the warrior maiden, Camilla.'

Flora nodded her thanks, and wondered briefly how she was ever going to go back to her normal life. *Do I even want it?* she thought. *When this is over – if we all survive – perhaps I could stay in the Silver Kingdom, and be a knight of the queen* . . . She looked at Johnny. Would he want to stay? Would she miss her family and friends?

The legionaries were readying themselves. They formed up into two small cohorts of one hundred and fifty men each, in ten lines of fifteen, leaving two lines of one hundred and twenty-five to come in after them. When they marched, they would lock their shields together so that their line was impenetrable. If attacked from above, they could raise their shields too.

Simon and Johnny stood side by side in the second rank of the left cohort; on the other side were Flora and Pike, both tense and ready.

'At my signal, then,' said Cautes calmly.

The filly was at his side, her velvety nose sniffing the air. The eagle, on her perch, appeared as unmoving as stone.

Cautes spoke, his words translated by Gaius. 'We will attack these knights, and we will overcome them! Fight for Rome! Fight for your families! Fight for home!'

The men roared and banged their shields.

The two vanguards prepared themselves, moving apart swiftly, confidently. The Roman legionaries were firm, their discipline overcoming any fear they might have. The sun was high above them, pitiless and hot. In their armour they sweated; their weapons heavy in their hands.

No one knew what they were going to face exactly, Simon realised. Things not even alive; shadows, but substantial nevertheless. What would become of them if they died at their hand, in this place?

To die in a world within the worlds, to become nothing at the centre of the universe. He pushed the dizzying thoughts away from his mind and tried to focus on his body. *I can feel myself,* he thought. *That is what is important right now. I can feel each limb, each nerve, each blood vessel. My heart is pumping. I am alive. And I am going to stay that way.*

He turned to Johnny and they clasped hands firmly. 'I'll have your back,' said Johnny.

'I know you will,' answered Simon. He looked across at Pike and Flora, and a moment of togetherness passed between them.

Cautes surveyed the scene below as they moved. The replicant army waited, the black knights in ranks with their weapons beside them; ravaging royal hounds sniffing about hungrily between the cohorts; the replicant King Selenus staring straight ahead.

'Ready?' said Cautes. The attackers drew to a halt in position, and tensed.

Simon closed his eyes and uttered a prayer. He knew now to whom he was praying. The goddess, in her cave. 'Help us,' he muttered under his breath. 'Help us. Help us win through, and reach home.' He thought about rain there, pure and clean on his face. The sea washing on to the beach. A swan gliding down to the water – a swan that was just a swan and nothing else. His mother reading a newspaper in a striped old deck chair. His father fumbling for his keys in his trouser pocket.

After a pause that seemed to stretch for aeons, Cautes snapped his arm downwards.

The two cohorts ran, pouring down the shallow, scrubby slope into the plain beneath, quickly covering the thousand paces before the edge of the army began, their pace long and steady.

Simon's cohort was breaking into the army from the left. His armour bounced uncomfortably. He could see little to the sides under his helmet, and it rubbed against his forehead. He coughed, and shifted the hunting horn so that it didn't jiggle quite so much.

Then, before he knew it, Marcus was roaring a battle cry in front of him, and swiping with his sword at a knight.

They were among the enemy ranks.

The left vanguard, tightly packed together, ploughed through the enemy's edges, knocking aside the black-armoured knights who'd been polishing their swords and helmets. They barely had time to pick up their weapons or put on their armour properly. The legionary in front of Simon entered into combat with a tall knight who was taken by surprise, and quickly fell. When he touched the ground, he slumped, and then his body dissolved into black smoke, dispersing into the air.

'*Imagines!*' shouted the legionary. Ghosts. The Romans, roaring, redoubled their efforts.

Simon felt the hunting horn buzzing at his side,

humming with life. Johnny was fighting hand to hand with a young squire, their swords clashing, the squire toying with Johnny. Simon didn't have time to go and help him; a legionary fell at his side, and he found himself face to face with a grinning, armoured knight pacing slowly and heavily towards him, and waving a mace above his head.

Meanwhile, on the right flank, Pike was slashing his way through, slicing here to the left, there to a tendon, here into an exposed abdomen, there to a neck. Swathes of black smoke followed his progress.

Flora, grasping the sunsword, had entered into a new kind of consciousness. She was completely unaware of anything around her, except for the sword and whoever it was connecting with. It was as if the sword had become an extension of her body.

As they approached the centre, she could hear its voice whispering more strongly in the back of her mind. *Keep going*, it was saying. *You are almost there.*

The priest Marcus was a good fighter, stabbing and slashing, roaring as he went, leading his men into skirmishes, pressing always on towards the replicant King Selenus. A royal hound hared towards him, jaws slavering; he dispatched it without even looking.

They were cutting a line from both flanks

towards the centre, but the knights had now taken up their weapons, and began to close in on the two wings from the back. Eight legionaries fell, laid low by knights. They lay wounded or dying on the ground, their groans piercing the air.

Watching from above, Cautes sent the first reserves onwards. They charged as swiftly as they could manage, and fell upon the knights with vigour.

All was steel and brightness and clashing, black smoke coiling into the wind. The battle cries of the knights filled the air, their glossy black helmet plumes flowing backwards as they ran, swords aloft, smashing into the legionaries.

Simon ducked the mace arcing down on him; it missed him by the smallest breadth of air. As the knight rebalanced himself, Simon turned and blew the hunting horn desperately. Though weak, the force of the sound was enough to knock the knight backwards. Panting, Simon rushed onwards behind Marcus. Johnny beat back the squire and swung round, gasping for breath; he caught sight of Simon and followed.

Despite the numbers being against them, they were winning. Simon felt the elation of battle in his bones, his blood singing with the fight. He rushed against a knight and dispatched him, then spun round to catch another coming from behind. Side by side with Johnny, he followed in Marcus's wake.

A cheer came from the legionaries of the first reserves. They had routed the knights; now the left and right vanguards joined together.

They were almost at the centre of the plain now. Almost where the replicant king stood, grinning a red smile at the carnage around him. The remaining knights formed a circle around him, lances bristling like a hedgehog.

Bellona whistled, and her whip came down on the Roman soldiers, knocking ten of them flat to the ground. One or two lay there, lifeless and broken. The others struggled to right themselves.

Cautes made the sign to regroup. The legionaries, with the friends among them, formed up into ranks, shields locked in front of them and over their heads, facing the enemy, and the king in their middle.

Aiming again with her whip, Bellona cackled.

Simon began praying. Would the legionaries' shields take the force of her whip? He didn't have time to think about it more, as she cracked it down on top of them. The group shivered, but held.

Gaius shouted the command to move forwards,

and the tortoise formation drove on. They had to stay tight, and push a line through the remaining knights; the other legionaries would come down and take out the flanks.

At least, that was the plan.

As they approached the front rank of knights, Bellona flicked her whip again, and tore off three shields from the arms of legionaries, who yelled in pain and fell, crushed by their own comrades.

The tortoise formation broke up. The fighters were exposed, and the huge and ravening form of Bellona looked down upon them. The remaining knights charged.

'She's just like the others,' shouted Pike. 'She can be hurt!'

Simon dodged a blow from a replicant knight, and nodded at Pike. They had to get to Bellona. But how? He stabbed at the knight, and was almost pushed back by the force of the knight's response.

The whip came down again, so close to Simon that it nearly unbalanced him.

Flora ran gasping to Simon's side and steadied him.

'What do we do?' yelled Simon. 'We need to stop Bellona.'

'I don't know how!' answered Flora. Around them the battle raged; the whip poised above them like an enormous snake.

When it next came down, unthinkingly Flora clamped on to it, and held on grimly. It was as thick as a tree trunk.

Simon, getting the idea, jumped on the whip next to Flora and clung tightly, pulling it down with as much force as he could muster.

Bellona screamed, and tried to push Simon off. But Johnny came dashing up, and stabbed at her giant left hand with his sword, before seizing the whip too.

'We've almost got it!' shouted Simon.

Pike turned from where he'd just dispatched another knight, and sprinted over to join them, bounding from about ten paces away and clinging on to the whip where Johnny stood, straining.

'Together!' shouted Flora.

They tugged hard, pulling on the whip, Pike slashing at Bellona's left hand so that she couldn't use it to brush them off. The giantess's face was distorted with anger, her eyes blazing, her mouth dripping with blood and foam.

Simon freed one of his hands and stabbed

Bellona's lower arm with his sword. They all yanked at the same time, came tumbling away holding the whip, and fell to the plain in a confused heap.

Bellona stamped her foot and reached down with her left hand, but Johnny was too quick for her and ran it through with his sword. The sword stuck unpleasantly in the gristle, and Johnny could not pull it out.

Meanwhile Gaius and Marcus joined the attack with a group of legionaries. They went for Bellona's feet, stabbing at her calves and lower body. Gaius, buoyed by the success of their tactics, leaped upwards, and slashed into her side.

Bellona let out a grim shriek and then slowly tottered, falling to the ground even as she began to dissolve into liquid black smoke, which coiled and grasped at them as they scattered away from her. With a final, savage movement, Bellona's whip struck Gaius full on the side of his head, breaking his neck, and the commander of the Roman forces fell lifeless to the ground.

About five hundred replicant knights remained and three hundred legionaries. The numbers were getting more even. The legionaries called to each other, picking up weapons from where they'd fallen, reforming into tight lines. Pike led Johnny to the second line, where Flora and Simon joined them, shaken but encouraged by their encounter with Bellona.

Marcus was now their leader. They had no time to mourn, no time to fetch Gaius's body. The two armies faced each other across a small space of ground the width of five swords. Cautes watched from above. The filly whickered her nostrils. The eagle arched her neck.

Behind the replicant king rose the home of the goddess, the dark stones on top of the hill like empty eyes gazing out.

There was silence, and then a trumpet sounded from the enemy ranks.

There was movement behind the knights surrounding the king. Simon could see flashes of shadow, glimmers of red.

Then the replicant king shouted, and the knights released the vicious royal hounds. They roared in anticipation of blood, their jaws foaming, claws tearing up the ground as they ran at the legionaries full pelt.

Chapter Eighteen

BATTLE
RAGES

A GREAT BARKING went up to the sky as the wave of ravening hounds hurtled towards them. The legionaries stood firm, but the dogs bounded over the front line and began to snap and snarl their way through the ranks like an unstoppable flood – hundreds of hounds with red eyes and bared fangs. Simon stabbed one in the back as it went past; his sword stuck into it for a second before the beast dissolved, but not before the hound had swiped at his arm with its claw, and left a long, bleeding wound that made the sword harder to grasp.

Flora was dissolving hounds to the left and right

with the sunsword, and Simon ran to join her.

Meanwhile Pike was facing four hounds that were circling him, their hot breath and ripe stink powerful. The largest jumped as he charged at it, met him midair, roaring ferociously, and sank its teeth into his shoulder where they met the metal of his armour.

The beast, undaunted, clung on, and Pike sprawled to the ground. As another came running at the young knight, he threw a short dagger at it, catching it in the side and pinning it down.

Johnny was beset, hardly able to hold off the pair attacking him, each thrust bringing those horrific jaws closer to him.

Simon was on his knees, trying to bat off a hound that had knocked over Flora. The legionaries were being swamped, and the knights were taking the advantage.

There was a hissing and a sharp squeal, then a thud, and the hound on top of Flora lumbered over.

Two more hisses followed in quick succession, and a hound fell by Johnny, and another at Pike's feet.

It was Cautes. Cautes shooting arrows down into the battle, his aim steady and true.

'Quick!' yelled Pike, and there was a flurry of

movement. Swords flashed in the air. The sunsword, buzzing, slashed through a hound's flank; bodies fell to the ground. For a moment there seemed to be nothing but rank fur and blood and the terrifying red eyes of the hounds.

Cautes was firing one arrow after the other now, hounds falling to the ground everywhere and dissolving into smoke. The leader of the hounds' pack, sensing a new danger, turned its sights upon Cautes, and the remaining hounds surged towards him. The legionaries ran at them from behind and, roaring, picked them off until the final one, the leader, was impaled and vanished in a thick fug of black smoke.

Now the friends were in the thick of battle once more. Johnny, sword flailing, was set upon by a knight, their line now advancing. He blocked the knight's blow and was momentarily elated as he smashed the knight's head, dizzying his enemy.

It did not last long. The knight soon recovered, shaking his heavy helmeted head from side to side, and went for Johnny.

Johnny was spending all his energy stabbing at the knight, who blocked his stings at the last minute. Too late he realised the knight was toying with him, laying in low, easily deflected blows, waiting to tire him out.

Meanwhile Pike was thrusting forwards towards the replicant king. He saw that there were four knights guarding him, one facing each way. The one right in front of him was the replicant Knight of the Swan.

Pike had long lived with the idea of revenge. His own father had been killed by King Selenus with the help of the Knight of the Swan. And his revenge had been taken away from him when the knight had killed himself in the square, after the king had died.

The thought had been quietly gnawing away at Pike's mind. And now, when he saw the Knight of the Swan, replicant though he was, something snapped in his brain, and he became filled with thoughts of his father, of death, of the knight, of the unfairness of everything.

A royal hound growled, hackles raised, and jumped at his throat; Pike dispatched it coolly, his focus never wavering from the replicant Sir Mark, the Knight of the Swan.

Johnny was to Pike's right, the replicant black knight still teasing him, and Johnny's arms were beginning to weary. All sorts of images flashed in front of his eyes, but every time he tried to summon his strength and push back, he found his limbs weakening, his mind losing its focus.

A blow to the head took him unawares and he tottered, falling to his knees. He looked up at the black knight now facing down on him, about to take his life.

With a final thrust, Johnny heaved himself upwards, and stuck his sword right into the gap between the knight's cuirass and the plates that covered his upper thighs. The black knight looked down momentarily, before aiming a blow at Johnny's arms. Johnny released his sword and jumped away, landing heavily and rolling over, jumping up and grabbing the hilt of the sword where it was stuck into the knight, and pushing it in with all his might.

This time the knight faltered and fell. Flora, spying her brother, came to his aid, yelling with all the might of battle in her blood. As she arrived, Johnny pulled out the sword, and they were enveloped in the black fug. When the smoke dispersed, they looked at each other over the empty space where the knight had been. They did not say anything, but they clasped arms, their faces bloodied and sweaty, set with a new kind of certitude.

'To the king!' shouted Flora, and Johnny yelled in triumph. 'To the king!'

When they reached the circle of knights, they found Pike there already. Simon arrived just behind them, gasping. The legionaries and knights around them were engaged in a series of small skirmishes, but the legionaries had gained the upper hand, and the knights were vanishing in their thick black smoke.

Marcus appeared, panting, with a small group of legionaries, who formed a protective circle around the four friends. Attacked by two knights, they began fighting. The clank of their swords resounded in the air.

Pike was facing the Knight of the Swan, and behind him, the replicant king who neither moved nor spoke, fixed them with his red glare, a cruel sneer on his face.

'I challenge you!' shouted Pike. He was weeping, he realised, and he wiped away his tears. 'Sir Mark, Knight of the Swan! I challenge you to combat under the laws of the Silver Kingdom! You killed my father . . .'

The replicant Knight of the Swan, immobile, might as well have been made out of wax.

Pike yelled in frustration and went to attack him, running as fast as he could and bringing his sword round in a circle. The other three knights in the king's guard simply stepped towards the replicant Knight of the Swan, and all four presented arms to Pike.

This did not stop him, and he ran onwards, blindly, towards the pointing swords.

'What shall we do?' said Simon. 'He'll be killed! Stuck like a pig!' He pulled the hunting horn to his lips, but before he could draw breath, Pike was among the four knights. He spun on his feet, clashing swords with one of the knights, then immediately darted to the left and parried a stroke from another. Simon could not look away, and was unable to focus the horn's power. The replicant Knight of the Swan was twisting his sword in his grip, hanging back from the fray.

All the while the replicant king sat on his horse, tall and proud, his red lips pulled back in a horrible grin, cape billowing about him, cruel horns pointing upwards from his head. Everything about him was exactly the same as the original king – except for his eyes, which were black.

Skipping to the right, Pike thrust backwards and sliced the tendons of a knight's legs; the knight fell, and Pike jumped over his body and took another knight by surprise in the neck.

This left two. One black knight, and the replicant Knight of the Swan.

Pike came face to face with the black knight. He feinted to the right, and then as soon as the knight moved to block him, he swapped sword hands and cleaved through the knight's protective armlet.

Slightly stunned by the blow, the knight dropped his sword, and Pike ran him through with a stroke that took almost all of his strength.

He had enough left, though, to face the replicant Knight of the Swan. He pulled the sword out of the dead knight's body, and wiped the reeking black stickiness off it. Then he stood his ground and squared up to his enemy.

The replicant clapped his hands together and bowed ironically. And then he came in for the kill.

The knight's movements were a blur, faster than the eye could process. The knight sliced into Pike with a hefty swing, connecting with Pike's soft flank. Pike howled and the knight stepped back, ready to make the final stroke.

Suddenly, Marcus ran forwards from where he'd been fighting close by, and tried to deflect the blow the knight was making at Pike.

But he slipped, and before anyone could do anything, the replicant Knight of the Swan had slain Marcus. Pike gasped in horror.

The knight, grinning, turned back towards Pike. Simon placed the horn to his lips and was about to blow.

Then a voice came, loud over the clashing swords.

'Father?' A tall teenage boy came walking softly, picking over the fallen bodies of the legionaries. It was Cygnet.

The replicant Knight of the Swan looked away from Pike.

'What are you doing here?' said Cygnet.

The replicant knight, annoyed at being interrupted, turned towards Cygnet fully.

Cygnet walked past the others, entirely focused on the replicant Knight of the Swan. He did not see the king behind, did not see the black smoke of the replicants billowing around them. All he could see was his father, who he'd thought dead, now alive and in front of him.

Pike groaned in pain, and Flora ran to him quickly, stemming the flow of blood with a piece of cloth torn from her dress.

'You are in the way,' said the replicant Knight of the Swan. 'Move aside so that this knight can be finished.' He pulled his sword out of Marcus's body.

'Father!' called Cygnet, almost running now.

'It's not your father!' called Simon, coming to help Pike and shielding him.

Cygnet paid him no heed. He moved closer. 'Father, you are alive . . . I did not know. You could have called me, left a message for me – I would have come to you!'

He went nearer, hands outstretched, the locket swinging from his grip. The replicant Knight of the Swan bowed low and grinned. Cygnet held the locket out towards him, an expression of joy across his features.

'You are alive, Father! After all this time! And I am here now, Father, with you! I can join you. Together we can avenge Selenus! You always taught me about honour and duty – I will do mine now!'

He came within an arm's length of the replicant knight, who, still grinning, balanced his sword in his hands. Then, with the swiftness of a hawk darting to kill a running hare, the Knight of the Swan struck a blow at Cygnet's head.

Instinctively, Cygnet put up his arms, and the

blow glanced off his armour.

'Father?' said Cygnet, uncertainty brimming in his voice. He lowered his arms slowly, surprise evident in his face. 'Is this a test? Are you . . . are you testing my loyalty?' His expression changed, setting solid. 'If so, then I am ready for it! I am ready to show you that I am loyal to you!'

Simon pulled himself up from the ground, covered the space between him and Cygnet as fast as he could, and interposed himself and his shield between Cygnet and the knight as the sword clattered down, in what would have been a killing stroke.

Cygnet rolled away from Simon and spat, 'What are you doing?'

Simon struggled to parry the knight's blows.

'It isn't him!' called Flora. 'It's a replicant! A shadow being! This whole army of knights isn't real!'

'I don't believe it!' shouted Cygnet.

'Look at his eyes!' Flora called.

Cygnet did, and saw only black and empty orbs.

'It cannot be . . .' said Cygnet, as Simon raised his shield once more against the knight. 'I thought you were alive.'

A change came over him. His face contorted through pain and horror, and then resolve. He looked around at the scene – the legions fighting the knights; Cautes above, and what had been his father about to kill the boy who had saved his life.

The Knight of the Swan had pinned Simon down now. Simon, weak and helpless, was unable to push him off.

Cygnet rushed towards them, and held his sword up above the replicant knight. He paused for only an infinitesimal amount of time, before he steeled himself, and sliced through the arm that the replicant Knight of the Swan was bringing down upon Simon, turned and, with everything he had, delivered a mighty sword stroke, piercing his armour and his heart.

Then he paused, and watched as the replicant dissolved into black smoke.

Cygnet knelt on the ground as the dark billows curled around him before vanishing into the air, and tears streamed down his face as he sobbed like a child.

Chapter Nineteen

THE CENTRE
OF THE WORLDS

NOBODY WENT NEAR the young knight.
Nobody dared. He flung his sword away,
and buried his face in his hands, his whole body
trembling. He fumbled with the straps of his helmet,
ripping it off, and then he planted his head in the
grass.

Simon approached him, but Cygnet yelled out
when he came near. Simon faltered, unsure what
to do, when Cautes came galloping down towards
them from his vantage point at the top of the hill, the
eagle on his wrist, the filly alongside him, and Anna
mounted behind him, clinging on, an expression of

grim determination on her face, her hair blowing back in the wind.

The small army of legionaries had slowly found its way back into formation, having ended the last of the replicant knights. There were many casualties on the Roman side, and the cries of men in pain filled the air.

But their task was not yet finished.

The replicant king remained, still mounted on his horned horse, still gazing imperiously down at them, still unmoving, and still between them and the hill of the goddess.

Cautes pulled up his horse and dismounted. Anna jumped off behind him. Her doll was slung around her neck in a sash, and she pulled her out now. 'We've come to help,' she said fiercely.

Cautes surveyed the scene. There was Cygnet, now prone and unmoving; Simon, standing near him, sweating and tired; Flora kneeling by Pike and tending to his wound; Pike's face contorted in agony; Johnny, exhausted and panting.

The eagle and the filly had gained in weight and presence, the filly now almost as high as Cautes's horse. But as the eagle and the filly approached, the substance of the replicant king shifted and stretched.

He grew larger, and the shadow around him flowed towards the watchers.

Horrified, the group stepped backwards, as the replicant king's substance swallowed up the body of Marcus where it lay.

The replicant king laughed, his cruel eyes shining, and he reared his horse upwards, before landing powerfully and launching towards the companions, the horse's hooves tearing up the turf.

'Stay back!' called Cautes. 'Avoid the shadow!'

'There is no escape,' came a voice from the replicant. 'You have come so far. Yet you will not be able to pass me.' His sword blazed, and he slew one of the legionaries. He turned his horse around and pranced in front of them, up and down, as if daring them.

'Don't approach him!' shouted Cautes, as Simon and Flora started to move.

'Then what shall we do?'

Cautes began to glow with the radiance of the Golden Realm, and to walk forwards to meet the replicant king.

But the blackness met him, and it was only with a huge effort that he managed to shine enough to push it away. He fell back, holding on to Simon for support. 'I do not know what to do . . .' said Cautes. 'This remnant of him is too strong . . .'

Simon blew the horn suddenly, but the note rang out ineffectively. Flora pulled out the sunsword and slashed at a tendril of blackness; nothing happened.

The replicant king considered them all. 'Now, which one shall I take first?' he said. 'A demi-god, weakened, at the foot of the house of the goddess? Now that would be a fine thing.' And he charged at Cautes, sword raised, shadow swirling towards him.

The blackness began to envelop Cautes, and the sword was coming down on to his neck.

The king's eyes flashed.

As swift as thought, something swooped down and tore the sword from the replicant king's grasp, dropping it a few paces away.

It was the eagle. The shadow withdrew; the eagle dashed herself against the replicant king, and the filly galloped up beside her.

The two met, forming a brief arch over the neck of the king's horse.

That connection made a glowing light. The light grew, and filled the space between their arch, covering the replicant king.

The shadowy stuff the king was made from

fought against the light, suppressing it, absorbing it. The eagle and the filly started to tremble; their connection broke and the light vanished.

With a huge effort the filly reached forwards and touched the eagle, and a new burst of light came from the joined pair, swallowing the darkness; thick black smoke absorbed into the brightness.

There was nothing left now of the replicant king.

In triumph, the eagle took wing and soared over the hill of the goddess; the barrier had gone, and she swooped in wide circles around the standing stones, before returning and settling down with the filly, exhausted. The two breathed gently in unison.

'The king's shadow is gone!' said Cautes. He cheered, his golden voice ringing around the plain, and everyone joined in. Pike banged his sword against his shield, and Johnny did the same; soon the whole army was banging their swords, the din and the joyful shouts mingling and echoing.

The cheers came to an end, naturally, and they began to tend to the wounded and the dying. The Roman soldiers, without their commander and their priest, were demoralised and hopeless, but Cautes spoke to them, and appointed Decius, one of the younger centurions, as the new commander. The words he said to them gave them hope; he pointed to the eagle, and Decius bowed reverently to her, then to Cautes. Cautes nodded in return.

'We will leave them here,' said Cautes to the others. 'They will bury their dead, and form a guard to the entrance, in case there is anything left behind of the foe. Now we must reach the goddess herself.'

'Are we all going?' said Johnny. He had recovered, and a new expression transformed his face, no longer looking weak and gaunt, but hardened, his eyes alert and keen.

'I will lead,' said Cautes. 'And then Simon, you follow with Pike and Flora.'

'But what about –' started Johnny.

'You, Johnny, will also come – you will be Anna's special guard.'

'Anna? Is she coming too?' said Simon.

Cautes nodded, thoughtfully. 'Yes. When we reach the goddess, we will want her with us when we are sent back.'

Anna merely looked at the ground, eyes shadowed, face drawn, and clutched her doll. Johnny went to join her, and instead of saying that she didn't need looking after, she put out her hand, and

Johnny took it and smiled at her. Simon nodded, and then joined Flora and Pike, the three of them once more forming a unit, each one wounded, bandaged, sore and grim-faced.

The end of their quest was there between them, its rough edges rubbing against them, and they knew that whatever form it took, they would be in it together.

They clasped hands. The eagle raised her head, then rose and flew in a lazy circle around them. They released each other.

'Ready?' said Flora.

'Ready,' answered Pike and Simon.

'Wait . . .' came a voice. A quiet voice.

Cygnet had pulled himself up from the ground, and was now sitting with his hands on his knees. 'I have seen many strange things,' he said. 'I do not know now what is real or what is not, but I know that I want to come with you. I want to see everything. I am compelled, and there is nothing else for me.'

Simon went forwards and offered his hand. Cygnet took it, and they held each other's gaze for a second.

'You saved my life,' said Cygnet.

'I did what I had to do,' answered Simon.

'I am bound to you now,' said Cygnet quietly as Simon released his hand.

'I accept your pledge,' said Simon. 'Will you help us reach the goddess, and return to our home?'

'I will,' said Cygnet, and they gripped each other's forearms.

'Good. Now, let us go,' said Cautes. 'We have quite a climb ahead of us.'

The sides of the hill were steep and rocky. There was no obvious path, but Cautes went ahead, sure-footedly. He was ravaged, the battle having taken it out of him, but he stepped upwards with dogged perseverance, tugging at tufts and rocks, and making sure that the way was safe.

Simon pulled himself up behind Cautes. Flora was whistling a low tune behind him, and Pike was steadily making his way. Johnny had put Anna on his shoulders, where she perched, holding on to him tightly. The eagle had vanished, but the filly was scrabbling her way up with them, just ahead of Cautes. Her nostrils were flaring with eagerness, her ears twitching. Cygnet kept up the rear.

The air was beginning to get cold, and they could see their breath as they climbed. The sun was moving to their right, and the circle of stones above them cast a shadow that seemed to stretch and spread down towards them as they climbed.

Soon they were in the shadow, and the fire of the legionaries was a small speck below them. It was now genuinely, unnaturally, cold, and their teeth began to chatter. They were not dressed for it. Simon had the clothes he'd come in; he gave his jumper to Anna, and Flora put on Johnny's leather jacket.

'It feels like we are halfway there,' said Cautes. But the stone circle at the entrance of the goddess's cave seemed as far away as it had ever been.

They carried on climbing, and the sun began to sink. The filly scampered up ahead, and disappeared over a low brow. When they crested it, they could not see her anywhere. The stone circle loomed above them, still so far out of reach.

Cautes faltered. 'I thought this was the right way, that the filly was guiding us,' he whispered to Simon.

They were all shivering now, and Johnny slung Anna down from his shoulders and pulled her into his side, supporting her as they climbed.

The sky above them was darkening, and little

stars appeared in the heavens. A shooting star went rocketing past, and they all gazed up at it. There was a strange corona around the moon, appearing now silver and huge, colours bright like the aurora borealis around it.

They clambered onwards. Hunger was a distant memory. Their energy came from somewhere else, as if the goddess herself was keeping them going. Flora could feel the sunsword gently buzzing, louder than ever. The horn around Simon's neck was vibrating, so much so that it was keeping him warm.

From the stone circle suddenly came a flare of light, and with it a sound, booming across them and down the hillside. It washed over them like a rush of wind, and they held on to the ground, fingers gripped into the cold earth to hold their position. The colours around the moon flared. When it had passed, Cautes said joyfully, 'The three are reunited! But she is still bound, and if she is bound, her other aspects are bound too.'

The way was becoming steeper now, and the hillside was almost vertical. They pulled themselves up, inch by cruel inch.

When there seemed like there might be no end

to it, the hill levelled out, and they came tumbling on to a small plateau. There stood the stone circle, emanating a warm golden light. A sound like the song of a whale was drifting towards them.

They trudged across the plateau. Flora unsheathed the sunsword; it flared more brightly than it had done for a while, providing them with light, and they followed in its path.

Staying close together, they crossed the remainder of the plateau.

Within a few minutes they had reached the entrance to the cave of the Threefold Goddess. It was huge, a plain black door rising up above them, set into one of the monoliths of the stone circle that stretched out round the whole summit.

As they neared the door they saw that it wasn't plain at all. In fact, it was alive with shimmering intricate patterns, all weaving and coiling in and out of each other.

They stood staring at that black adamantine door, so vast.

It had been there since the beginning of time; it would be there at the end of time.

Simon felt as if he would be able to stand there looking at it and its shifting patterns for ever. It didn't seem to matter if it opened or not. It took up the entirety of his brain: all thoughts of home, and everything else, had vanished.

Cautes paced to the door and placed his palm on it, a light glow coming from his hand.

Something creaked, and slowly, with the sound of stone scraping on stone, the door moved on its hinges, and opened a way into the blackness at the Centre of the Worlds.

'Simon, blow your horn,' said Cautes. 'We must announce our presence.'

And Simon put the horn to his lips and blew. The sound of the note rang out clear and pure, clearer and purer than he had ever heard it. The horn was coming home, and it knew it.

This was the centre of everything. Here were all beginnings, all endings; here was all meaning.

Dauntless, not knowing what they would find, the little band passed through. The door closed firmly behind them as they entered the corridors of the home of the goddess.

Chapter Twenty

THE
THREEFOLD GODDESS

A CORRIDOR OF stone, sloping downwards, wide enough for ten people to walk abreast, opened before them, lit at intervals by guttering torches. The whale-like song cascaded down the passageway towards them. Eerie and enticing, it urged them onwards.

Cautes was glowing, his face and hair emitting a golden sheen. The sunsword was almost back to its full power. Flora could hear it singing now, the voice that had been gently humming always at the back of her mind, adding to that enthralling whale song, echoing and repeating and twisting in on itself.

The hunting horn was doing the same, and Flora and Simon joined together, held hands, and the voices of their weapons grew louder.

'They are coming home!' shouted Simon.

The corridor came to an end, and in front of them was a huge stone chamber. There were three thrones at the far end of it, and three figures seated upon them. A golden aura surrounded the two at either edge, which faded towards the figure in the centre.

Two of the figures rose as the band entered. They were women: one in a long, dark, feathered dress, who shook out a pair of huge wings as they entered; the other wore white, and her long, long hair fell about her like a grey horse's mane.

The third figure was indistinct, small and hunched up. She was writhing, a low pain-filled cry coming from her. Around her was a peculiar darkness.

Cautes came forwards, signalling to the others to stay where they were.

'My goddess,' he said. 'What has happened to you? What can we do?'

'You see,' said the mare and the eagle as one, 'what has happened to our sister. She lies here, still trapped. King Selenus used ancient powers and stole a part of her for his shadow. We cannot reach her.'

The mare goddess bent forwards, and tried to stroke the hair of her sister. Her golden aura went dark, and she pulled her hand back in shock. An invisible barrier prevented her from getting any closer.

'Do not come near,' said the mare and the eagle in unison, as the little band approached their thrones. 'No living person can come near us. You will be destroyed.'

Cautes retreated. 'I am Cautes, a supporter of Mithras.'

'We know who you are,' said the mare and the eagle as one. 'You are one of our favoured persons. We feel that Mithras is empty, though you and his followers remain. You are strong and powerful, and yet still you may not come near us.'

Flora's sunsword was humming audibly now. As in a dream, she held it out in front of her. It was glowing all down its length, like a sheet of liquid fire. Her grip loosened on the hilt, and everybody watched in amazement as the sword left her grasp and floated towards the eagle goddess, who took it smoothly and stood up from her throne, holding it vertically. At the same time, Simon's horn detached itself from his body, and floated to the mare goddess. Their auras brightened perceptibly as they rejoined with their weapons.

Yet the third, central figure still groaned and thrashed.

'These weapons have returned to us,' said the mare and the eagle. 'You have borne them well, Simon Goldhawk and Flora Williamson. You have been pawns, all this time, in greater games. But you have shown yourselves true and good. And now . . .'

The mare and the eagle reached over the central figure and held hands, creating an archway of shimmering brightness. But still the shadowy goddess writhed in pain.

'Even with the horn and the sunsword, we cannot mend her,' they said. 'King Selenus maimed her when he took the substance from her robe.' Their brightness dimmed as they parted. 'The worlds are twisting and breaking as she perishes.'

The mare and the eagle knelt on either side of their maimed sister.

'This is what he tore from her,' they said, and spread out a filmy, black, shadowy substance. 'King Selenus came here, he spoke dread words, and he maimed the goddess herself. He trapped us. The shadow came back to us when he died, but it has his words on it still, parting it from her, stopping her from becoming whole.'

'How did he maim her?' asked Cautes.

'We cannot speak the words. They are the words of the unmaker. The words of the serpent.'

Simon remembered the vision he'd had of the three goddesses and the snake. 'It's all one,' he murmured.

'Death and life and life and death,' said the mare and the eagle. 'Here everything comes together. And we are out of balance.'

Cautes looked stricken. Pike was standing with Cygnet: the two resembled each other, in their armour. Simon had his arms around Anna, and Flora was linked to Johnny, clutching each other.

'King Selenus was the serpent,' said Cautes.

'Yes,' replied the mare and the eagle. 'The agent of destruction. All must be destroyed, for all to be born anew.'

The walls of the house of the Threefold Goddess began to tremble.

'Wait . . . Are you saying you're giving up?' exclaimed Flora. 'That all of this − all of us − will be destroyed?'

The walls of the house of the Threefold Goddess began to tremble.

'And no one can save us?'

There was no reply save the rumbling of rock. A crack appeared in the ground not far from where they were standing. The thrones of the goddesses themselves began to shake. The mare and the eagle closed their eyes.

'Cautes!' said Simon. 'What shall we do?'

They held hands in a circle, all of them, and faced each other. The things that they had seen went unspoken between them as the crack widened and the roof of the cave began to shiver, sending down showers of scree.

The thoughtless wishes that had brought Simon and Flora here burned in their minds along with stolen siblings, golden messengers, shadow-snakes, burning swords and other worlds. A chunk of stone landed by the foot of the goddesses.

And all of it, all of the strange, rich, unknowable mess that was the universe, was going to die. The glass pyramid of the Temple of the Threefold Goddess, shattered; the queen's palace in the capital city, ruined; their cottage in Limerton, destroyed, and everything else that would ever exist.

'Close your eyes,' said Cautes. 'And I will sing, and we will not witness the end . . .'

The song that haunted the stone corridors rose from the mouths of the eagle and the mare, as their sister, hunched and powerless, wailed and shrieked.

The friends closed their eyes, and Cautes began to sing. He called their names, each in turn. Johnny. Cygnet. Flora. Simon. And each in turn answered, as the megaliths around them shook in their foundations.

'Anna,' called Cautes, in his song.

But there was no answer.

'Anna!'

They opened their eyes.

Anna, seeming impossibly small, was steadily climbing the steps towards the Threefold Goddess. She was holding her doll, and the last shadow-sphere.

Simon broke the circle, and shouted, 'What are you doing? You'll die if you approach them!'

'I'll die anyway!' shouted Anna back over her shoulder. Ignoring his protests, she continued. Simon moved to run, but Cautes restrained him.

'Get back!' Simon called.

Anna stumbled a little, then righted herself,

looking only at the ground ahead of her.

Helplessly Simon struggled against Cautes as Anna reached the edge of the aura that swathed the goddesses. They regarded her, infinitely distant, the mare and the eagle, and the woman who lay bundled and broken.

Simon cried out, but his cry faltered, and died on his lips.

Anna was standing at the edge of the circle of the goddess. In front of her, the maimed goddess, lying frail and weak, crumpled on her huge black throne. Anna held out her doll, pulled out a scrap of paper, and said some words, which made Cautes look sharply at her.

'The library!' said Cautes. 'She found it in the library!'

'What?' said Simon.

'Leave her be – watch!'

The goddesses stretched out the shadowy substance.

And the doll moved, and yawned, and Anna placed it down on to the top step, and gave the shadow-sphere to the doll. With a look of triumph, Anna folded up the paper, and nudged the doll in the direction of the goddesses.

The doll, looking about, seemed to know what to do. It took the needle from its waist, and walked into the aura of the goddesses.

The little band broke their circle, and crowded on the steps of the thrones, gazing up.

The doll stretched out the shadow-sphere to a thin thread, passing it through its hairpin sword, using them to stitch the torn shadow to the goddess. She stitched busily. She pricked her finger, but carried on, stitching the length of the torn substance. The robe was not simply a piece of clothing, it was part of the goddess herself.

And as the doll sewed, the goddess gained in power, the aura glowing brighter. The eagle goddess lifted the sunsword and a great light came from it; the mare goddess blew her horn, and the noise seeped through the room, as warm as the sun.

When it was fixed, the doll ran over the lines of stitches once more.

At once the auras of the goddess expanded.

'Anna! Get out of there!' yelled Simon.

As if coming out of a trance, Anna snapped her head around, and her eyes widened in terror. 'My doll!' she cried.

The doll had fallen, inert, and was just inside the

aura. Anna went to get it, but was pushed forcefully backwards.

Simon leaped up the steps to meet her as she came hurtling down. Their hands grabbed for each other and they went tumbling to the stone floor, falling into the others, knocking them into a heap, just as the aura of the Threefold Goddess flared violently.

'Out! Out!' shouted Cautes.

Scrambling to their feet, they rushed back into the stone corridor.

Running, following Cautes, they tumbled out into the night air, and down the hill, which now seemed small and easy, and into the remnants of the Roman camp. The legionaries surged around them, gaping and staring up at the stone circle. It was now full of golden light spilling out from the stones. They paused, and turned to watch what was happening.

'Anna! What on earth did you do?' said Simon, breathlessly hugging her tightly.

Anna answered. 'Found a spell in the library for my doll to come to life. Then I heard you all talking about shadows and I remembered the sphere and I thought maybe the shadow-sphere was the same thing as the goddess's shadow.' Then, overcome with shyness and exhaustion, she went mute, and hugged Simon instead.

'Well done, Anna! Well done!' said Cautes. 'Your sister,' he continued, turning to Simon, 'has just saved the three worlds!'

Anna smiled, then fainted in Simon's arms, and he laid her gently on the ground. 'Water, quickly!'

As he tended her, the stones of the circle fell as one, and from the ruins rose a gigantic, shining woman, swathed in swirling white robes. She looked about her. The moon rose, and the sun rose also, and yet behind her they could see the stars. The whole plain was flooded with light.

She sang a note, so beautiful it thrilled every cell in their bodies. She pointed at the Romans and the whole legion vanished, back to where they had come from, where they would make their way to Rome with tales of goddesses and other worlds.

Looking at the little band she said, 'We thank you. I am free. No living thing could have approached us. But the doll was not alive, and Anna was its bearer. And now I sing!'

She sang. All their lives afterwards, none of them ever forgot what they heard. When they were old, and their memories were fading, and they were not sure if what they had seen and done was a dream or a fantasy, they all remembered what the goddess sang.

It was love and power and creation, but in it was a deep, melancholy strain that rang like a clear bell. Around them the plain sprang into life. From over the hill came She-who-rakes-the-shores with her children. Even a swarm of hideous insects came to buzz and listen. They were all her creatures, and they all fitted into her dance, her song, her dream, her life.

'There is much for me to do,' she said, when her song had finished. 'And now I open the Way for you.'

In the air appeared a gap, and through it they saw the library of the Temple of the Threefold Goddess in Boreas, and Arion, staring at them, surprised and elated.

The goddess roared. She became an eagle, and a lion, and a mare, and a snake, and though the snake hissed and reared and spat, they knew it would do them no harm, and she was all of these things at once.

Anna came to, and Simon lifted her gently into his arms. For a moment it was as if the little group were not separate units of being, but joined and whole.

They were everything, and everything was in them.

'So all things are eternal,' said the Threefold

Goddess. 'So all things stream into one another, falling through the void, coming together and falling apart. Now go.'

They stepped through the gap, one by one, into the library where they had left Arion and Mithras, and where, exhausted, they stood and looked behind them as the gap sealed itself. Each sank to the floor, closed their eyes, and passed into a sleep as deep as time itself.

Chapter Twenty-One

MONKEYS

SIMON WAS THE first to wake. He sat up hurriedly and reached on instinct for a weapon. Then, seeing the rows of books and the light streaming through the windows, he realised where he was, relaxed, and blinked.

The small, friendly features of Arion, the young priest of Boreas, were looming over him. He was holding out a wooden beaker, in which was something hot and spicily scented. Simon grabbed it, gulped it down, and was immediately revitalised.

Arion then went round the rest of the group, handing them beakers from a wooden tray. Pike woke clutching his dagger. Flora and Johnny both stretched, yawned, caught sight of each other, and laughed at the same time at the state they were in. Cautes woke more gently, simply opening his eyes. Cygnet was limp and floppy; he turned away from the others. Anna, jumping to her feet, ran straight at Arion and hugged him, kissing him firmly on the cheek.

Arion blushed, and when she had finished he said, 'You all have to come with me. Something strange has happened.'

Feeling that nothing could be stranger than what they'd seen so far, the group of adventurers followed Arion into the main pyramidal body of the temple, where they were met by a living tableau.

Sun came through the glass panels of the pyramid. The two monkey creatures, in their much torn clothes, were standing in the centre of the temple.

They were holding someone in between them, who was bound in ropes and covered in sacking.

'I do not know what to do with them. I do not understand them. They arrived this morning. I fear they mean harm,' said Arion.

Cautes stepped forwards and spoke to them.

'Honoured guests,' he said. 'Do you please take some rest, some water, and some food?'

They growled and lifted the sacking from the third person, and Pike let out a gasp. There, her mouth gagged, bruised and bloodied, was the Lady of the Snake, Pike's mother. She struggled when she saw Pike.

Cautes said imperiously, 'Do you please release my sister and friend, the Lady of the Snake.'

The larger creature chattered, and made gestures that suggested they would kill her.

Pike grabbed his sword and was about to rush them, when Cautes said, 'No! Something is afoot here. We will find it out.' He continued more gently. 'I give you my word as a supporter of the demi-god Mithras, that we will not harm you, and that we will help you in any way that we can. Only do you please release my sister first.'

The monkey creatures turned to each other and spoke in their guttural noises; then, coming to an agreement, they nodded, and to the amazement of all, the larger one spoke, in a hoarse voice, as if every word was difficult. 'We cannot give her up until we have what we need.' The creature wheezed, and spat, and grinned.

Cautes motioned to Arion to bring them seats. They sat, warily, still holding the lady between them.

Something struck Simon as he gazed at their torn clothing. He studied them carefully, and looked for confirmation of what he thought. Then, quietly, he slipped away and found his possessions. Delving into his rucksack, he pulled something out and returned.

When he showed it to the pair, they began talking excitedly. The larger creature stretched out his hand tentatively, and Simon nodded.

'Wait!' said Cautes. 'What is it?'

It was the button – the button that they had used to get into the holding place under the supermarket right at the start of their adventure.

'Where did you get this?' said Cautes.

'I've had it all along,' said Simon. 'We found it in a clearing near where I live.'

'It is ours,' said the leader of the two. 'Give it to me, and I will release the Lady of the Snake.'

Cautes regarded them thoughtfully. Then he said, 'Do it, Simon.'

Simon gave him the button, and the monkey creature took it with glee, and as he took it, it changed into a golden amulet. The two creatures grasped each other, and knelt; then immediately unbound Pike's mother. She ran, sobbing, to her son, and they embraced. Cygnet looked in the other direction.

'What happened to you?' asked Pike.

The Lady of the Snake shushed him, and said, 'Time enough for that later.'

Cautes, laughing, said, 'I have never seen such a thing!'

The leader said, 'Home. This will bring us home.' And without another word, the two creatures swept out of the room, bounding like monkeys. Everyone rushed after them, but they had already vanished from sight, heading back towards whatever mysterious place they had come from.

'How did their talisman get to you?' asked Cautes when they had returned to the pyramid.

'I can answer that,' said the Lady of the Snake. 'The Silver Princess stole that talisman from the king, and gave it to me, and I left it for Flora and Simon.'

In high spirits, they sat down to eat a meal of the sweet, sharp fruits, which they gathered from the gardens and the orchards, and when they had rested, and eaten, and rested again, Cautes asked Arion quietly what had happened to Mithras.

Arion shrugged, saying that he did not know, and that soon after the rest of them had entered the realm of the Threefold Goddess, Mithras had disappeared.

At this, Cautes frowned. 'There has been no communication? No magehawks? Nothing?' Arion shook his head, and Cautes said, 'I fear that he may have gone from this world,' but when pressed, he said nothing more.

Later, as the sun set, Simon was outside and noticed Cautes on his own. He was kneeling and staring up at the sun, and held out his arms as if he wanted to be taken up and burned in its rays. His eyes had no expression, and Simon let him be.

They slept that night in the chambers of the priests. Anna insisted on sharing with Simon, and he let her. She curled up into his side, a little bundle of exhausted girl, and slept soundly. Simon lay awake for a long time, thinking over what they had done, and dreaming of what was to come.

The next day, the whole party set off back to the capital. Arion had found the local villagers were gradually returning to the temple for news. Some of them were opening their farms and homesteads again, and he managed to buy enough horned horses for all of them.

When they were due to leave, they sent a magehawk ahead to Selena; as it shivered its wings and vanished, Arion ran down the front steps of the temple, the glass pyramid glinting in the sun behind him. 'I'm coming with you. The temple can look after itself for a while.'

Anna said quietly, 'Will you ride with me?'

And Arion, looking very pleased, said he would.

It was warming up as they gradually made their way into the lands towards the capital city and the direction of the south wind, and the Port of Notus. The roads were busier and they met several travellers, though they could get no coherent report from anyone as to what was happening in the capital. Some said that the new queen Selena reigned strong; others that there was dissent and strife. They never saw a knight, or a squire, or a lady; only merchants and farmers and labourers.

One thing that all they passed agreed on was that the boundaries of the land were strong again. There were no stories of strange beasts or decaying forests in the far reaches.

Cautes was in a quiet mood, but that did not prevent them all gasping with joy when they passed through the hills and on to the main road to the city, and were met by a whole train of travellers, who sold them a sheep. They gathered wood and lit a huge, crackling fire. Pike and his mother prepared it, and they got it on to a spit, roasting it whole.

It took a long time, but when it was ready, they ate and drank greedily, enjoying it as if they had never eaten before.

Cygnet sat apart. He was curt and brusque whenever anyone tried to talk to him. The others, sensing his troubles, left him alone. Always he played with the locket around his neck, opening and shutting it, touching the lock of hair that had come from his own head when he was a little boy.

Onwards they rode, as quickly as they were able. Pike was deep in conversation with his mother; Johnny took his place next to Cautes, asking him question after question about the worlds and the way they had come into being. Flora, smiling and quiet, went along beside him. Anna and Arion guided their little ponies side by side, sometimes galloping ahead for sheer joy, sometimes ambling alongside Simon.

Cygnet came by himself, at the rear, keeping

look out, and saying not a word.

Soon the black glass towers of the capital city rose ahead of them in the distance. Flags and pennants were fluttering from all along the walls.

As they approached, a shadow shifted, and a magehawk appeared and settled on Cautes's saddle. He quickly took its message, read it, and a line appeared on his forehead.

'We must hurry. There is trouble ahead.'

Chapter Twenty-Two

THE

FINAL FIGHT

THE GATES TO the city were open as the little group made its way inside. No guards stood to check them, no residents came to greet them. The streets were curiously empty, and there was a dead silence.

Picking up the pace, Cautes went first. And then, as they approached the square, a knight staggered into the road in front of him. Reaching out a mailed hand, he fell to the ground, an arrow in his back.

'Arion, Anna, you stay here,' said Cautes. 'And no arguing about it.'

The rest of them formed into a close unit of three

by two, weapons drawn. Flora felt a sudden tug of longing for the sunsword. They approached at a gentle trot, and came around a corner into the great square, right into the middle of a skirmish.

Queen Selena was standing on the steps of the palace, sword drawn, looking down upon the fight. The Knight of the Hawk and the Lady of the Stag were fully in the thick of it. The queen was shouting orders.

The enemy forces, all in the black armour of the king's supporters, were led by Sir Ursus the Black Lion and swarmed up the steps of the palace. The queen's bodyguard surrounded her, lances pointing outwards.

Without waiting a moment, Cautes led the charge, and the six of them galloped into the fray. Johnny let out a war cry, surprising himself as much as any of the others, and Flora joined in. Whooping like crazy, the pair hurled their horses at the rebel knights. As Flora swung down and her sword connected with a black knight's, she felt the shock shiver all the way up her arm. She realised suddenly that this was true battle, and she no longer had the sunsword to protect her.

The black knight, noticing her minute faltering,

pushed the advantage, and almost toppled her off her horse. But Johnny roared to her defence, and brought his horse in between Flora and the attacker, knocking him out of the way.

Together the Williamson siblings yelled in triumph, sunlight glinting off the blades of their swords.

Queen Selena's guard was pushing back the black knights when Simon and Pike thundered towards them, Cygnet at their side. A thud of bodies followed their progress.

Then one of the black knights spotted Cygnet, and called out, 'It is the Cygnet! The son of the Knight of the Swan! Sir Mark's child! He is here for us!' The black knights cheered.

Cygnet reined in his horse, his face pale and drawn.

'He has come to lead us against the queen!' called another rebel. 'We will succeed! We will avenge King Selenus!'

Watching the queen intently, Cygnet said nothing. Simon had cut a swathe through a band of four rebel knights. Pike was chasing after their leader, Sir Ursus; Cautes had reached the queen and had joined her bodyguard, ready to defend her.

'Come on, Cygnet!' called a hoarse voice. All the black knights took up his name, banging their weapons in time to their chant. 'Cygnet! Cygnet!'

The shouts gave them new vigour. Dazed, Cygnet watched the battle. 'Wait!' he shouted. 'Stop!'

He moved his horse from side to side. Nobody listened to him.

Panicking, he jumped off his horse and entered the melee. He ran to where Pike was facing up to Sir Ursus.

'You're in for it now,' snarled Sir Ursus to Pike.

Pike looked, astonished, at Cygnet. There was a moment of pure stillness between them, before Cygnet, in a flash of passion, called, 'For the queen!' and hurled himself at Sir Ursus.

They clashed with a ringing of metal, and Cygnet threw himself into the hand-to-hand combat. Pike turned to block another rebel coming from the side.

A cold fury was possessing Cygnet. He thrashed and hacked, all of his careful training vanishing as he became a vortex of whirling limbs. Sometimes the black visor he was facing seemed to be that of his father and he weakened, but when he heard the rough voice of Sir Ursus, he redoubled his efforts.

He nicked Sir Ursus on the neck with a

backstroke, and righted himself so that they were once more face to face.

Sir Ursus laughed. 'Traitor, are you? To your father?'

It was the wrong thing to say. Everything that had boiled up in Cygnet now burst over, and he roared with rage and fury.

Sir Ursus never knew what hit him.

The rebels, meanwhile, had lost their focus. The queen's guard, led by Cautes, was rounding up the rebel knights.

Cygnet's hair was slicked back with sweat, and he was bloodied and panting. Bending over Sir Ursus, Cygnet removed his enemy's helmet, and hefted his sword, ready to kill.

Sir Ursus smiled at him mockingly. 'Whelp,' spat the Black Lion. 'Imp. Useless son of a noble father.'

Cygnet was about to strike, but then as he looked at that cruel, spiteful face, something clicked in his brain. Slowly, he put down his sword, and turned to where the queen stood.

'A prize for my queen,' he said, bowing. 'The rebel leader. For you to try, according to the laws of the kingdom.'

Then everything became blurred. Shadows

crossed through Cygnet's mind. The queen was shifting in and out of focus. He felt a sharp stab of pain, and looked down to see Sir Ursus grinning up at him, and the hilt of a dagger sticking out of his side. There was a great confusion of noise, and the city square swayed from side to side, and everyone was now looking down at him, all their faces merging into one terrible black-visored face.

Cygnet fell to the ground, his blood pumping out of him in gouts.

'Take him in, quickly,' shouted Selena, as Cautes sprinted towards them from the back, disarmed Sir Ursus and pushed him to the ground. 'To the infirmary!'

Simon rushed towards where Cygnet lay and lifted off his helmet. He was still awake.

Pike grasped the young knight's hand. 'Hurry!'

Hefting him up, Simon and Pike bore him up the steps into the palace, leaving Cautes and the others in the square. They took him to a cool, white room, where they undressed him, and a nurse shooed them away, before pressing a tourniquet on to his wound.

'Will he live?' asked Simon as they left. But the nurse simply closed the door, and the last they heard was Cygnet's cry of pain.

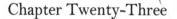

Chapter Twenty-Three

THE

HIND

'STOP IT! THAT HURTS!'

'I was only playing . . .'

Arion and Anna were chasing each other across the thickly carpeted floor of the queen's small private chamber. Most of the group of travellers had gathered there, and those who were lightly wounded were being tended, and they were all drinking long hot draughts of spiced wine. Simon was busily telling Selena what had happened after she'd left them.

As he spoke, Selena's face grew more and more full of wonder, until she clasped her hand over her mouth and gasped with surprise.

They had done it. They had entered the Centre of the Worlds, and brought the Threefold Goddess to her full glory.

They had broken the king's revenge.

When Simon had finished speaking, there was a long pause. He looked bashfully at the ground, and cleared his throat.

Selena glanced at Anna, busily employed in pinching Arion's cheeks and pretending he was a baby, something which Arion seemed not to mind too much. 'He said something to me – Mithras, before we left. He said he'd had a vision, and that it was unclear, but that it was from the goddess and that it involved Anna and her doll. That was why we had to bring her.'

She called Anna to her side, and, bending down, gave her a hug. 'You have done well, my child,' she said, and Anna, wriggling, escaped to Simon. She showed them a scrap of paper torn from the book in the priests' library – on it was a puppet, dancing. 'You see? I said I could do some of it but you wouldn't listen to me.' Simon ruffled her hair and she didn't pull away, but hugged him instead.

'And now it is time,' continued Selena. 'The

worlds are settling and the balance is being restored. We may open the Way, to let you back.'

'Can we come back here?' said Anna.

'Or go to the Golden Realm!' said Flora, looking at Cautes. 'I would love to see it.'

'Me too,' said Johnny. 'Take us!'

'You must return home now,' said Cautes. 'It is right. We have still much to do here now, and in the realm, to settle things properly. Prepare yourselves now to take leave of the Silver Kingdom, and the Golden Realm.'

'For ever?' said Simon.

Cautes shrugged. 'Perhaps not. But for now, at least.'

They went back to the rooms they had taken, and found laid out on their beds their remaining possessions. Anna squealed with delight as she discovered a new doll, in the shape of Selena, complete with horns and a long red robe. Johnny, who had arrived in the kingdom dressed only in his boxer shorts, found them there, along with a shirt made of fine silver material and a pair of white trousers. He put them on, enjoying the feel of the cool, odd clothes.

The porcupine spine was still in Simon's rucksack.

He showed it to Anna, who smiled at him, and they remembered the afternoon on holiday in Italy when she'd given it to him. Simon decided not to tell her that he'd used it to poke the eye of a royal hound.

Shaking out the bag, he found the pencil stub that had let them in to the holding place where the sunsword was kept.

On each of their beds was also a small crystal ball, which they assumed were presents from Selena. Simon lifted one to his eye, and looked at the others through it. They appeared dim and shadowy, but he saw nothing else. He slipped it into his pocket and forgot about it.

The five of them returned along the black glass corridors to the great hall of the palace, where the queen was waiting with Cautes, attended by a dozen knights and ladies. Lavinia, the Lady of the Stag, grinned at them, along with the handsome young Knight of the Hawk, on whose wrist perched a fine-looking goshawk, which preened as they entered and swooped around the room before returning to his arm.

'How's Cygnet?' asked Anna.

'In the infirmary,' answered Selena.

'Will he . . . will he live?'

'That I do not know,' said Selena. 'We are grateful to him, and he has done us great service.'

'He was a fine knight, my queen,' said Pike. They were silent for a moment, and Anna sobbed a little.

'He *was* nice to me,' said Anna.

'There is no need to cry,' said a voice, and Cygnet entered, limping, looking uncomfortable in ornate white ceremonial armour. 'I have recovered, my queen,' he said. 'It was but a scratch.'

'That was no scratch,' said Pike. 'You fought well.' Pike grasped Cygnet's hand, and the two young knights acknowledged each other. When Pike released him, Cygnet nodded briefly, catching Simon's eye.

Anna danced over to him, curtseyed, then ran off, suddenly embarrassed. Cygnet called her to him, and she returned, and Cygnet knelt down. 'I am sorry, my lady, for what I planned to do. Know that I will always be at your service, for the rest of your life.'

'Good,' gurgled Anna, and then to everyone's astonishment she kissed him on the cheek.

Cygnet smiled and took his place next to Pike, who was looking knightly and solid. Scarlet, the daughter of the Crimson Knight, who had helped them in the rebellion, was on Pike's other side, her hands entwined with his, and her eyes were bright and smiling.

Arion was wearing a long priestly gown embroidered with symbols of the north wind. He looked decidedly uncomfortable, but he brightened when he saw Anna.

When Simon offered the pencil to the queen, she looked at it for a brief moment, then said, 'Keep it. You never know what else it might open. We may have need of it yet.' At a sign from her attendant, Clara, the queen picked up silver garlands of flowers, and placed one on each of their heads, whispering words which made them glow with happiness.

Cautes led them down the great stairs. When the doors into the main square opened, they found a space filled with people and flowers. Everything was covered in garlands: the statues, the balconies, the heads of the men and women, and the people threw flowers at them as they passed. The whole populace of the city was thronging the streets, children perched on their parents' backs, dogs ran through people's legs. A squire and his lady on a horned horse went by them and she blew them a kiss. Simon caught a glimpse of Lucia, the Lady of the Pass, but she was gone before he could say anything, swallowed up in the rejoicing rush.

Soon they went through the city gates, now standing open, and the two royal guards bowed them out to a joyous fanfare of trumpets that sprang from the battlements.

As they walked towards the standing stone just outside the city, a great mass of shadows appeared beside them, and a flock of magehawks emerged, swirling into view, dropping messages into their hands. Cautes caught a few, and read them out. 'News of your deeds has spread far,' he said. *Thank you*, the messages said. *Thank you*. From the farthest reaches of the kingdom the magehawks came, swimming in and out of the shadows, and all of them bore the same message: *thank you* – from the Port of Notus and the Hall of the Sundering; from Selena's sisters in the Tower of Eurus; from the frozen settlements in the regions of Far Boreas; from across the seas the messages came.

The whole of the city it seemed followed them out on to the plain. Huge barrels of spiced wine, open and steaming, were placed along the route so all could dip their beakers in and drink in the bright silver sun. The magehawks vanished, sliding into the shadows, as Queen Selena led them all to the standing stone.

There the courtiers made a ring, with Cautes and Selena standing side by side. Arion was given a place of honour by Selena, and Pike and Cygnet, newly appointed as her royal bodyguards, were on either side of her. Cautes and Cautopates, reunited, were standing with their arms around each other's necks.

Around them were the knights and ladies of the court, and further beyond were the people of the city, all mixing together, all calling and laughing. A juggler was throwing coloured balls into the air; a magician was pulling shadows into shapes; another was blowing red, silver and blue flames from his mouth. The scent of roasting nuts and meats mixed with the general joyful hubbub.

'I give thanks,' called Selena, 'to those who have seen what none have seen before, save the king my father.' Her voice was quiet for the last few words. She looked about the throng, which was silent too now, save for the occasional bark of a dog, and a child somewhere, laughing. Selena composed herself, and resumed her speech. 'I give thanks to those who have set this kingdom aright, and who have restored the three worlds to balance. There is nothing I can say, nothing I can do, that can reward you fully. Know that you have our eternal gratitude, and that the Silver Kingdom, and the Golden Realm, will remember you always.'

Flora sniffed, and Johnny wiped his nose. Simon and Anna held hands.

'I will open the Way now,' said Cautes. 'You will return to your world, and my companions and I will go back to the Realm. We too cannot give you thanks enough. Your reward will come – when it is prepared. Now, are you ready?' He smiled at each in turn, and each felt that familiar warmth radiating through them.

The four siblings nodded, and held hands, circling around the standing stone.

Pike coughed, and Simon broke his grip. He ran to him, and even in his armour, gave him a hug, and Pike returned it. Then Flora came dashing over, and the three of them held each other, and for a moment there was nobody but them, and they said nothing, but listened to each other's hot breathing.

'I will never forget you,' said Simon, after a moment.

'Nor me,' said Flora, and kissed Pike on the cheek. She held his hand for a moment, then let it drop, and looked at Simon. 'I can't believe we're actually going now. I keep thinking he'll be back.'

'The king?' said Simon. 'I know.'

Cygnet extended his hand, and said, 'I have learned many things. I have seen strangeness beyond what I knew. But now I have seen goodness, true goodness. My father was wrong, but he was loyal to his king. And I will be loyal to my queen, in the right way. I will atone for what he did.'

Simon shook his hand, and Flora too. There was a little squeal, and Anna came running up to Cygnet, and hurled herself into his arms. The young knight held her apart for a second, then he drew her in, and she buried her face in his shoulder.

'Keep the crystal spheres safe,' Selena whispered to them. 'Tell no one of them. And one day you will know their function.'

Cautes began intoning the ceremony of opening, and as the gash formed in the air, the people of the capital city roared with excitement. The forest clearing in Sussex could be seen, sun spearing through the leaves.

One by one, they stepped through, Johnny first, then Anna. Flora and Simon went last, together, and as they passed over the threshold, they turned, and saw Queen Selena, her horns glowing silver, and Cautes, emanating a golden glow, and Pike and Cygnet, and they paused. Cygnet nodded once, and held up a hand in farewell. Pike, Knight of the Shark, smiled and bowed low.

And so they passed back into their own world, and felt the solid dry Sussex earth beneath their feet.

The gap in the air closed as quickly as it had opened, and they were left, so near to other worlds, and yet so far away.

The sun was up. It was early on a summer morning. The air was cool and fresh.

They started walking. There was a humming in the air, strange and high. Anna held on to Simon's hand. 'I'm frightened,' she whispered.

'Don't be,' said Simon.

The leaves all turned gold as they walked, and rustled with breezes that were not there. Something moved in the bushes beside them, and a great hind came out in front of them, and regarded them. Flowers sprang from where her hooves hit the ground, and they knew that it was the goddess. She came forwards and touched each of them with her muzzle, and they felt a sweetness fill their minds, inexpressible and pure.

They took their silver garlands off, and put them in Simon's rucksack.

Simon remembered the way that they had come, and he led them through the woods, over streams and down brackeny paths, the way clearer and brighter. They could not see the hind, but they felt her presence. They were not tired; they walked swiftly, and did not need to stop to drink.

Once Simon thought he caught a glimpse of something golden in the corner of his eye. He turned quickly, his heart beating; but it was only the sunlight on the surface of the stream.

They soon came to the field behind the Goldhawks' cottage.

'We'll go on to Moreton from here,' said Flora, a catch in her voice.

'This isn't goodbye,' said Simon, feeling tears welling up behind his eyes. He looked at Flora – reliable, clever, generous, witty Flora – and felt that here was another sister.

'Why don't you call me or something?' said Flora. 'You know, on an actual phone. I . . . I don't know what to say.'

'You don't need to say anything,' said Simon, and they hugged.

They parted, Flora and Johnny soon disappearing into the fields.

They all knew it was not for ever, that soon they would come together again, and they would be able to sit and talk in the cool of the evening about the strange things that had happened to them which they could never share with anyone else. They were bound together by invisible threads, for life.

Simon took Anna's hand. His little sister, who he'd wished away, so long ago now, it seemed. She had been the one who saved the worlds. She had been the bravest, the strongest of all. He kissed her, and she wriggled away, giggling.

A swan crossed the sky over their heads, and they watched it fly away into the distance.

The familiar shape of the cottage arose in front of them. The gold shimmering haze had gone, and it was there, solid and real. They approached from the drive, with the sea and the cliffs beyond them. The front door was open, and they could dimly see inside.

As they came up the drive, their mother shot out in her red dressing gown, mobile phone clamped to her ear. She saw them, gasped, and said into the phone, 'They're here!'

She shut off the phone, and came running to them in her bare feet, scooping them into her embrace.

'Never do that again!' she said crossly, kissing them all the while. 'Your father's out looking for you! Where have you been? Look at you, you're filthy!'

Simon and Anna exchanged glances. Simon began speaking, but Anna cut over him.

'I . . . I wanted to go camping, and I woke Simon up, and he thought it would be fun if he went with me, so we went,' said Anna.

'I'm sorry I didn't leave a note,' said Simon, passing Anna a conspiratorial glance. 'How . . . how long have we been gone?'

Their mother looked at him strangely. 'You should have taken your phones, you sillies. We got back this morning about three, and you were both in bed. Then Anna didn't wake us up at her normal time, so I knew something was wrong. And you'd made a mess in the kitchen – pans everywhere, and the cheesegrater on the floor! What on earth you were using it for I have no idea. Go in, now, have a wash, both of you, for goodness' sake! And no treat today!'

There was a screeching of tyres, and a car came

up the drive. Their father parked it and barrelled out.

He was looking very stern, and was about to say something when he noticed something behind Simon. 'Look!' he said quietly. They all turned.

Behind them, in the field, was a hind. The same hind they'd seen in the forest.

The hind watched them, and Simon and Anna stood with their parents, watching her. She lifted her gentle, delicate head, and shook her snout; quickly and impishly she cavorted towards them. Then she made a movement, bending her head as if bowing. Just for a moment it seemed that she had a pair of golden wings, stretching out behind her, but maybe it was a trick of the light.

Then she turned, her fine nostrils sniffing the air, and before they knew it, she had trotted away, and vanished into the woods.

EPILOGUE

I N HIS ROOM in the cottage at Limerton, on the same afternoon that he'd returned from the Silver Kingdom, Simon lay on his comfortable, familiar bed, looking up at the ceiling, exhausted.

Turning over on to his front he felt something in his pocket, and pulled it out. It was the chain that Andaria had given him. Andaria, the green rider, who'd slain King Selenus. She'd asked him with her dying wish to return it to her parents. He held it for a long time without moving.

Later that day he began looking online for information. He found references to Harriet

Fielding, the girl from his world who had become Andaria in the Silver Kingdom. Harriet had gone missing in the 1960s, when she was five. *Time*, thought Simon. *Time is all stretched and bubbled. Sometimes it goes faster, sometimes it goes slower.* He looked up her parents, and discovered that only her mother was still alive; her father had died of cancer. There was no mention of a brother or sister, but there must have been one, thought Simon. There must have been a sibling who'd wished her away.

He called Flora. It was strange to hear her voice over the phone, and for a moment they were unsure how to speak to each other. After a second she said, 'My scar. It's gone.' That broke the tension.

'Mine too,' Simon said, and he told her what he'd found, and they arranged to meet in a week's time.

Vera Fielding, now in her late eighties, was in an old people's home in Kent. Johnny came in the car to pick Simon up, with Flora riding shotgun, and they drove silently to the small village where the home was.

They parked in the drive. The home was pleasant and large – it had clearly once been somebody's house. An old lady wandered with her zimmer frame across the lawn; another was being pushed in a wheelchair to sit beneath the spreading branches of a tall oak tree.

'What should we do?' said Flora eventually. 'If we give it to her, it will open up all sorts of questions we won't be able to answer. They never found a body – they'll reopen the case, and then there will be trouble.'

Simon twisted the bracelet in his hands. He whistled between his teeth. 'We said we'd give it to her parents. We should do what she asked. She killed the king. We owe it to her, no matter the consequences.'

Flora nodded, and the two of them got out of the car, leaving Johnny behind. He mouthed, 'Good luck,' as they left.

There was nobody at the door, so they went straight into the hall. Nurses barely gave them a glance as they wandered down the corridors. A reading group was taking place in the drawing room, and glasses of dark sherry were being put out on a tray. The residents' names were stencilled on the doors in large black letters.

Soon they came to one that read: *Mrs V Fielding.* It was slightly ajar, and through the gap they could see a well-dressed lady sitting on a bed, with a book open on her lap. Glancing at Simon, Flora pushed the door open and went in first.

'Harriet?' said Vera Fielding. She looked up, wreathed in smiles. 'Harriet!'

Simon followed Flora, and the two stood awkwardly in the tiny room. There was a picture of Harriet as a little girl on the windowsill. Other photographs stood around, one showing a mother and two little girls, and books lay everywhere. Fresh lilies in a vase stood on a wooden table littered with newspapers. Through the window was the tall oak tree, its branches shading the room.

Flora took the bracelet from Simon, and gave it gently to Vera Fielding. She clasped it, and a tear formed in her eye. 'I gave this to you,' she said. 'My darling Harriet. I gave it to you when you were four years old. I remember the day so well. You loved it, you wore it always, even in bed.' She reached out a hand and stroked Flora's hair. It was too much for her and she began weeping. 'You came back, Harriet!' Flora stood back, alarmed.

At this moment the door swung open and a nurse came in.

'Harriet's here!' said Vera. 'Look!'

The nurse smiled at Flora and Simon. 'Visiting?'

she said. Flora nodded, and swallowed. 'We . . . were just leaving.'

They went out, and as they departed, Flora turned to look back. Vera was clutching the bracelet, and as they left, the nurse put it on her wrist. 'There now,' said the nurse. 'Did you drop this?'

She saw Vera looking at the nurse, and heard her say, 'Harriet? Harriet! You came back!' Vera reached out a hand and stroked the nurse's hair back from her head.

They left, Johnny driving, the roads full of everyday traffic, people flowing to and fro. The three of them were sliding back into their lives, back into the rhythm of normality.

When they reached the cottage by the sea, Simon got out of the car.

Johnny and Flora drove off, Flora turning to wave, and Johnny lifted a finger from the wheel. Simon watched them go, as he had watched his parents drive off on the night he'd wished Anna away. He turned, and saw her sitting on the doorstep, idly playing with a hairband.

'Come on, Simon,' she said. 'Come and dance!'

She dragged him to the cliffs, laughing. He ran with her, and they joined hands by the rocks, with the sea glistening below, and they danced, the salty breeze kissing their skin, and the sun gleaming down on them.

Later that night, Johnny was awake, a single lamp illuminating his face as he leafed through his old philosophy books, underlining and questioning and highlighting; Flora was lying on her side, clutching her hand around an imaginary hilt, her eyelids fluttering with dreams; Anna, the girl who'd braved the Threefold Goddess and saved the universe, was slumbering amid her teddy bears; Simon, at last, heavily, sweetly, lay in deep sleep; and four crystal spheres, in drawers, in wardrobes, on shelves, hummed and glowed and shimmered and levitated slightly into the air.

They clicked and rolled, and for a brief moment, a golden face could be seen through them.

It was Mithras, smiling.

ACKNOWLEDGEMENTS

ANDREA REECE, MARTIN WEST and all at Troika; Melissa Hyder for her, as always, intelligent and patient copy edits; Sarah Naughton for a good and sensible read through; Tom Williams, who set the whole *Darkening Path* going; and to my wife, Tatiana von Preussen.

→ Discover ⇐
THE DARKENING PATH

Reader's notes for
THE DARKENING PATH
can be downloaded from
tinyurl.com/TDP-notes